"We're bein' invaded."

Jenna exchanged a smile with Beau, and dropped her voice. "Invaded by whom, Elmer?"

"Hippies. See that fella across the way there? The one with the black cap and orange hair? The one readin' the newspaper?"

Jenna's breath froze in her lungs as the man with the shaggy, orange-streaked blond hair and dark beard shadow slowly raised his head and seemed to stare straight at her. Cold fear drizzled down her spine and, like a deer in the headlights, she couldn't look away from his long face and pointed jaw—his narrow shoulders. Then the man tossed some bills on the table beside the paper, and a moment later, he was heading toward the door.

Jenna's rapid heartbeat began to ease a little as Elmer continued to speak. He *couldn't* have been Court—not dressed like that.

Her hand shook a little as she reached for her coffee, and her cup rattled against the saucer. Get a grip, she commanded herself, refusing to look up when she felt Beau's heavy gaze on her. Elmer's hippie was simply a man passing through, who'd stopped to get a meal and would be moving on. He wasn't a threat to her. He wasn't.

Books by Lauren Nichols

Love Inspired Suspense

Marked for Murder
On Deadly Ground
At Any Cost

LAUREN NICHOLS

From the time Waldenbooks bestselling author Lauren Nichols was able to read, there was a book in her hand—then later, in her mind. Happily, her first attempt at romance fiction was a finalist in RWA's Golden Heart Contest, and though she didn't win, she's been blessed to sell eight romance suspense novels, and dozens of romance, mystery and science-fiction short stories to national magazines.

When Lauren isn't working on a project or hanging out with her family and friends, she enjoys gardening, geocaching and traveling anywhere with her very best friend, her husband, Mike. Lauren loves to hear from readers. You can email her at lauren_nich@yahoo.com or through her website, www.laurennichols.com.

AT ANY COST

LAUREN NICHOLS

Love Inspired

Recycling programs
for this product may
not exist in your area.

LOVE INSPIRED BOOKS

ISBN-13: 978-0-373-44487-8

AT ANY COST

www.LoveInspiredBooks.com

Printed in U.S.A.

The Lord is my light and my salvation—whom shall I fear? The Lord is the stronghold of my life. Of whom shall I be afraid? In times of trouble He will shelter me; He will keep me safe in His Temple and make me secure on a high rock.

—*Psalms* 27:1, 5

For Ann McCauley, Lindsay Randall
and Karen Rose Smith for your unwavering
encouragement and friendship. I love you guys.

And always for Mike. You're my everything.

PROLOGUE

Impatient to begin, the man sat in an idling, early model beige sedan outside a diner advertising Wi-Fi, his features hidden behind tinted glasses, a knitted black watch cap pulled low on his forehead. Outside, the mid-November snow was blowing sideways, sending a chill through him despite the blast of heat coming through the car's vents. He abhorred his appearance, detested his scruff of a beard. But the deception was paramount to conceal his identity.

Scowling, he consulted his wristwatch, saw that it was 9:00 a.m., then turned to the woman beside him and handed her a disposable cell phone. Usually slender and strikingly attractive, she wasn't much to look at now—not the way she was dressed today. The bulky winter jacket, mousy wig and owlish glasses had leeched every ounce of her appeal. Ridiculous pewter peace sign earrings swung from her earlobes. He'd been told that she was a woman of many names and talents. In fact, he suspected that even the name she'd given him was an alias. But according to the man who'd introduced them—a friend of a friend of an acquaintance—she was worth every cent he was paying her.

Opening his laptop, he snagged an internet connection from the diner and located an online building supply house that carried top-of-the-line power tools. He turned the screen toward her—pointed out two items.

"Kindly order the planer and the radial arm saw—and tell the salesperson there's no rush. Regular delivery will be fine." A hint of sarcasm entered his tone. "I wouldn't want to drain Ms. Harper's bank account."

"No flowers this time?"

"No."

Smiling, the woman who'd given her name as Deirdre Alaimo tapped the company's number into the phone, then accepted the business card he offered. As she'd done with the three purchases she'd made late yesterday, "Deirdre" gave the salesperson who answered Jenna Harper's name and address, placed the order, then turned the business card over and read the credit card number scrawled on the back.

"And may I have those items delivered to a different address so I don't have to transport them myself?" she asked sweetly. "They're a gift for someone special."

The driver heard the salesman's booming reply. "Of course, Ms. Harper. Where would you like to have them sent?"

She read the name and address on the front of the card, then tucked it into her pocket. A minute later, she said a cordial thank-you, then ended the call and turned to her employer. "Another purchase?" she asked coyly.

"No, I believe four trips to the well will be sufficient." The driver closed the laptop, then swiveling around, he exchanged it for the small overnight bag lying on his backseat. He handed it to "Mrs. Audrey Bolton."

"Everything you'll need is inside. Twenty-five hundred dollars in cash—a small portion of which you shouldn't mind using for your accommodations—a plane ticket and another set of credentials." The driver removed his glasses and sent her a cold, blue stare. "Naturally, you will destroy 'Mrs. Bolton's' credit card and photo ID as soon as you've accomplished your task and contacted the others."

"I've been doing this for a long time," she said, returning his chilly look. "I don't make mistakes."

"Good." Turning his head, he stared through the windshield where heat poured from the defroster, melting swirling snowflakes on contact. "Goodbye, Deirdre."

"Deirdre" didn't reply. She simply got out of the car and shut the door. Lifting his gaze to the rearview mirror, the driver watched her walk back to her rented blue Ford, climb inside, then start the car and pull around him onto the street. Her brake lights flashed briefly as an old woman wearing a plastic rain bonnet hurried across the street in front of her. Then the car was swallowed up in windblown flurries and he was alone with his thoughts.

It was good to have money, the driver decided, turning on the wipers and easing away from the curb. A person with money could buy interesting services, do interesting things. Anything except reclaim what she'd taken from him—what he'd held most dear.

Now it would be his pleasure to return the favor.

ONE

At 10:30 a.m., Beau Travis drove up the slight incline to the small blacktopped parking lot beside the Blackberry Hill Bed and Breakfast and parked his truck. Wind-whipped snow flurries rode the crisp morning air. He wasn't a fan of snow, but in Pennsylvania's Allegheny Mountains, from mid-October on, it was only a matter of time until it showed up—and it was November now. Leaving his jacket on the seat, he swung out of his charcoal-gray Ford F-250, slammed the door and grabbed his heavy toolbox from the truck's bed. Wind tunneled down the neck of his navy sweatshirt as he hurried up the walk to the sprawling gingerbread-trimmed, pink-shingled Victorian's white porch. He preferred to get an earlier start on his jobs, but Jenna didn't like having her late-sleeping guests rousted from their dreams by power tools.

As always—particularly for the past two weeks since he'd been working here—Beau felt an airy anticipation in his gut as he stamped the snow from his boots, rang the bell and waited for someone to buzz him inside. The door latch clicked, and he entered. No way was he in the market for a relationship. But he was a thirty-six-year-old red-blooded American man, and he still enjoyed looking at a beautiful woman. Jenna Harper was that and a whole lot more.

He closed the glossy oak door with the side lights and etched glass inset behind him, then paused in the foyer where the registration desk took center stage. The aroma of freshly baked pastries filled the air. Jenna was on the phone, and in the second it took before he noted the anxiety in her eyes, his mind absorbed everything about her. Everything from the pretty sun streaks in her shoulder-length ash-blond hair, to the soft pinkish-lavender sweater she wore with cream-colored wool pants. Her tone and the nervous way she fingered the gold cross at her scooped neckline spiked his awareness.

"No. No, the charges aren't mine," she said. "I haven't used that credit card in two years. Are you certain this wasn't an accident? Someone could have juxtaposed the numbers when they—" Her voice rose shakily. "I see. How many charges were there?"

Beau took his time wiping his boots on the mat. This was none of his business, but he hesitated just the same. Generally, he kept his nose to the grindstone and his eyes straight ahead—didn't get involved in other people's concerns and kept his own little dramas to himself. But she was different. She intrigued him—had since she'd been an underclassman at their high school. She was incredibly beautiful, but didn't date. She was friendly, yet there was a wariness about her that she couldn't hide. She shared bits of her life, but quickly changed the subject when his questions approached anything close to personal. And now that he thought about it, he rarely saw her out and about except for Sunday services at St. John's.

When she spoke again, her voice trembled. "There

were flowers delivered to three different *funeral homes?*" She pressed her free hand to her stomach. "No. No, I don't have family members in those cities."

Nodding to her and receiving her tense nod in return, Beau followed the carpet runner past the formal parlor toward the dining room. Okay, she'd been the victim of identity theft. It was a growing crime, but most credit card companies didn't hold cardholders responsible for some hacker's criminal bent. But unless his radar was all messed up—or unless he was linking her reaction to her lifestyle—she was afraid. That made him afraid for her, and an unexpected jolt of protectiveness hit him squarely in the chest.

With a nod to Jenna's great-aunt Molly who was fussing with table settings beyond the dining room's French doors, Beau turned right, stepped through a doorway, and tried to focus on the sitting room he'd be restoring. He'd finished the bedroom upstairs. Today he needed to remove the molding and aging wallpaper in here, then size the walls. He scanned the room. The drapes were down, and snow blew past the long window that had been exposed. The sill would have to be replaced. He'd stored small pieces of furniture in the attic yesterday, then ripped up the carpeting and moved the larger furniture to the middle of the room. Jenna had draped them in plastic: two rose-colored camel-back settees, a highboy and a couple of small tables. He set his toolbox on the floor next to his Shop-Vac, then unable to shake his concern, glanced back through the doorway and the trouble he'd sensed at the front desk.

Tiny, feisty Molly Jennings strode inside, a pixie grin in place, her feathery cap cut as white as the flurries outside. "Late for breakfast again," she teased, shaking a bony finger. "What am I going to do with you?"

Beau chuckled. "I told you. I don't eat breakfast. I had a cup of coffee at the Quick Stop before I came over."

"A cup of coffee is no way for a big, strapping young man to start his day," she insisted, then linked her arm through his. "There are a few cranberry muffins left, and they'll just go to waste if you don't help me out." She continued before he could refuse again. "Besides, we still have an expectant mama upstairs who might like to sleep a little longer. She won't be able to do that once you start banging around in here."

Grinning, Beau let her drag him into the Victorian's dining room. Molly Jennings—who'd been "Aunt Molly" to him since she'd bailed him out of a mess during his teenage years—was singing the same song she sang every day when he walked in. Today he'd accept because he wanted to ask about Jenna. "Okay. I'll have a muffin if you do, too. Then I have to get to work."

Aunt Molly parked him at a table that was already set with cups, saucers and condiments, then scooted over to a courtesy table that held beverages for the Blackberry's guests, and grabbed a carafe. She plucked two muffins from the warming basket and put them on fancy china dishes.

Beau smiled, watching her add knives and pats of butter to the plates. She was still a pint-sized dynamo at eighty-something, and looked perfectly at home in a room outfitted with silk flowers, antique dolls and cream-and-roses wallpaper. As always, she wore period clothing and high-button shoes. Today's outfit was a floor-length dark green skirt and a high-necked, white blouse that puffed at the shoulder, then molded her matchstick arms down to the wrist. It was well known that from the time she'd opened the Blackberry Hill Bed and Breakfast fifty years ago, Molly Jennings had delighted in creating a slice of history for her guests. That hadn't changed after she'd sold the B and B to Jenna two years ago.

"Here you go." She handed him a plate, set hers down, then returned for the carafe. She carried it back to the table. "Now grab a chair and tell me what's on your mind."

With a curious tilt of his head, Beau pulled out her chair, waited for her to sit, then took the seat beside her. At six foot two, he was a giant sitting next to her four foot ten—a giant in a room too feminine and fussy for a man of his proportions. "Why do you think something's on my mind?"

"Because for the past two weeks, I've been trying to get you in here for breakfast, and until today, you've refused."

He grinned. "Maybe you just wore me down."

"And maybe I'm sweet sixteen and waiting for my prom date. Now, out with it."

He was trying to come up with a subtle way to ask why Jenna was so guarded about her past when she came inside. The agitated look in her wide blue eyes hadn't changed since that phone call.

"Good morning," she said, seeing him and quickly calling up a smile.

Beau stood. "Good morning."

"I see Aunt Molly finally nagged you into accepting some breakfast."

Molly headed back to the china cabinet, her reply

drifting airily. "I don't nag, dear, I simply suggest. Who was on the phone?"

Beau watched Jenna take an unsuccessful stab at nonchalance. "My credit card company. Apparently, someone has my account number, and they've been having a lot of fun at my expense. Literally."

There was no point in acting surprised. She knew he'd overheard part of her conversation. "I imagine the card company's investigating," he said.

"Yes. That's why they called. I guess when charges are made out of state on an account that's been dormant for two years, it raises a red flag."

There was a rattle of china as Molly fumbled with a cup and saucer, then smiling a little too brightly, she carried them to their table. "You cancelled the card, of course."

Jenna nodded soberly. "Yes, but I should've done it a long time ago. The woman who called said there could be charges that haven't posted yet, but they'll refuse payment. I'm not liable for them. As of now, my fraudulent friend's fun is over."

But Jenna was more upset than she should be, all things considered, and Molly seemed to be feeling a bit of that, too. Picking up his muffin, Beau wrapped it in a napkin and hid his concern behind a smile. It was time for him to leave. Jenna obviously needed to speak to her aunt alone. "That's good news. Glad things worked out." He nodded toward the open doors. "Now I need to get busy. You're not paying me to socialize."

Jenna hurried to put him at ease. "No, please stay and enjoy your breakfast. Don't let me chase you away."

"You're not," he said, forcing a chuckle. "The fear that I'll be pulled into a girl-talk session is." He shifted his attention to Aunt Molly. "I'll keep the noise down. Scout's honor. No power tools until noon."

But there was no feisty comeback from his tiny boss, only a smile and a nod—and his concern grew.

Jenna watched him go, then rose to close the French doors and turned to her aunt. She didn't like hearing the fear in her own voice, but there was no way to stop it. "It's him, Aunt Molly. I think it's him."

Molly's brow lined as she left her seat, then took Jenna's hand and guided her back to the table. She scooted her chair closer to Jenna's. "You don't know that. Identity theft is running rampant these days. It's all the talk on TV. Now, it's been two years, and he knows the police are looking for him. He wouldn't do anything to call attention to himself."

Jenna shook her head. "He has money. A lot of money. The man was the CEO of a huge financial conglomerate. People like Courtland can have things done without putting themselves at risk."

"That doesn't mean he can access his funds. The authorities have to be monitoring his accounts."

"They probably are, but it doesn't matter. He has funds elsewhere."

"Honey, you can't know that."

"But I do know it," she insisted. "He's a narcissist. He liked to impress me. He told me once that he only vacations in the Caymans to visit his money."

Molly took her hand again. "Jenny," she said softly. "This has to stop. Every time there's a hang-up call that's almost certainly from a telemarketer, or something a little out of the ordinary happens, you overreact. How could he find you? You never told him you were originally from Pennsylvania, so he has to believe that you're Michigan born and bred. And when you bought the Blackberry, you used a company name. Everything you buy goes on my credit card or you pay cash." She paused, then spoke again. "There's another possibility. Someone else who might want to torment you."

Jenna met her great-aunt's pale blue eyes. "Someone else? What are you talking about?"

"The Chandler trial."

That disturbing confrontation with the Chandlers came back to her and Jenna felt a rush of remorse again. She and the other jurors had deliberated long and hard before turning in their verdict. But she alone had been ambushed outside the county courthouse as she walked to her car because she'd spoken for the twelve. Devona Chandler had flown at her in a tearful frenzy while Lawrence Chandler stared darkly from a distance, looking every inch the executive he was in his tailored black topcoat and white scarf. Rattled, Jenna had quickened her steps.

"Mrs. Chandler, we shouldn't be talking."

"How could you have done this? Our Timmy's a good boy! He made a mistake! He didn't mean to hurt anyone!"

"Mrs. Chandler, please—"

"You could have convinced the others to show some compassion, but instead you turned a blind eye. There were extenuating circumstances!"

She'd known she shouldn't respond. But a young father of three had died because, for the third time, the Chandlers' partying, twenty-three-year-old son had been driving drunk, this time without a license.

"I'm sorry," she'd said sincerely. *"I truly am. I didn't want to find him guilty, but I had no choice."* In fact, throughout the proceedings, she'd prayed hard that God

would guide her decision when it came time to render a verdict. *"But I'm afraid the evidence was overwhelming. Actions have consequences."*

Tears rolling, the woman had turned around to send her husband a heartbroken look. Then she turned back, met Jenna's eyes again and said in a startlingly cold voice, *"They certainly do. And you're about to find that out."*

Jenna forced the memory away. Blaming the Chandlers was definitely preferable to the scenario she'd come up with, but it was easier to believe the worst. "That happened in the early spring. Why would they retaliate after all these months?"

"That's a very good question. Why would *Courtland Dane* do it after two years?"

Jenna drew a shaky breath. "I don't know. Maybe because he wasn't able to until now. Maybe he's been out of the country."

"Honey," Molly cautioned quietly. "You need to put this in perspective. We're talking about credit card fraud. No one's threatened you."

She realized that. But her aunt didn't see the danger because she didn't have all the facts. "Aunt Molly, whoever used my card number charged flowers—huge, expensive arrangements that were sent to funeral homes in three different cities. Boca Raton, Los Angeles and Boston. I—I made a few calls after I hung up with the credit card company. All three of the decedents were *Harpers*."

Molly paled, touched the cameo at her throat. "No."

"Yes. Now do you see why I think he's involved? This…this flower thing has Courtland's sly stamp all over it. Devona Chandler spoke out of grief for her son. It was his third DWI and a man died. She knew he'd go to prison. People say things they don't mean when they're in pain."

For a long moment, Molly seemed to gather her thoughts. Then she rose, murmured a quiet "Wait here," and went into the kitchen. When she returned, she was carrying a newspaper from the mudroom's recycle bin. She opened it to the second page, then handed it to Jenna.

"I set this aside when it came a few days ago because I thought it might upset you. You had some sleepless nights after the trial. Now, reading this might make you feel better."

Jenna accepted the paper, then glanced at the headline and smaller subtext below. Appeal Denied. No new trial for Timothy Chandler.

Molly spoke again. "You asked why the Chandlers would want to retaliate months after the trial," her aunt said gently. She squeezed Jenna's shoulder. "That's why."

It was a little before noon when Molly entered the sitting room to survey Beau's mess. The crown molding he'd been able to save was stacked against one wall, and the discarded chair rail lay at the back of the room among rolls of dusty, torn wallpaper. For some reason Beau couldn't comprehend, someone had recently replaced a lot of the original oak with cheap pine that hadn't come close to matching, and it, too, had to go. He found that odd, since Jenna insisted that the rooms in the hundred-and-thirty-year-old home be kept as close to original as possible.

"Not a pretty sight, is it?" he asked wryly.

"No, but it will be lovely when you're through." Molly frowned. "I just wish we'd hired you first. When a body's down on his luck and needs work, we're glad to help, but—" She stopped suddenly, then tapped a shushing finger to her thin lips and smiled again. "Forgive me. That wasn't kind. As I said, the room is going to be lovely."

"Thanks. I hope you're right." Beau waited for her to speak again. When she didn't, and instead took a slow walk around the scarred hardwood floor, he realized that she was working up to something. Her clunky heels echoed in the stripped-down room.

"Okay, it looks like it's my turn to ask what's on your mind," he said.

She didn't hedge. "The same thing that was on your mind earlier today. Jenna. She told me you probably overheard part of her conversation with the credit card company."

"Yes, I did." He didn't mention that some of what he'd overheard had been deliberate eavesdropping on his part. Wiping his hands on a rag, he walked over to Molly and dove into the conversation he'd wanted to have earlier. "She's unusually guarded. We've talked a little about high school and other things, but she never says much about her life after graduation—or why she didn't come back to Charity after college."

Molly stopped walking. "There was no good reason for her to return. Her mother moved back to Michigan after her father died, so Jenna naturally settled there."

Beau nodded. By that time, he'd served a couple of years in the military, finished trade school and was trying to build himself a life. "Jenna said she taught high school English in a Detroit suburb. I got the idea that she enjoyed it."

"And now you're wondering why she came back to

Charity when her mother, friends and a job she loved were hundreds of miles away."

"It crossed my mind."

Frowning, the tiny woman walked to a covered settee and settled lightly on the arm. "I won't tell you why. That information has to come from Jenna if she cares to share it. But I've seen the way you look at her. It's the same way you looked at her years ago when you were here doing my yard work. You like her."

An uneasy feeling crept in. That made him sound like a voyeur or a potential suitor, and he wasn't interested in being either. Better to set the record straight right now. "I care about her as a friend. If she's in trouble, I'll do what I can—but only if I'm asked to help."

"Well, that's not apt to happen," she said, sighing as she rose. She squared her thin shoulders and raised her chin. "So I'll be the one to ask. I need something from you."

He would never deny Molly Jennings anything. Not after all she'd done for him. "Whatever you want is yours. You know that."

"Thank you. I would like a bowl of Italian wedding soup from the diner. Takeout, not dine-in. It's the special today. I just spoke to Aggie Benson. She says it goes fast."

Beau stood flat-footed and bewildered, trying to link her request to the serious conversation they'd been having. Obviously, this wasn't about Italian wedding soup. After a moment, he realized what she wanted. "Why don't I ask Jenna if she can get away for lunch? We never discussed whether she wanted to re-carpet the floor in here, or if she'd rather have the hardwood refinished. If she decides she'd like to talk about something that's bothering her…maybe my reassurance would be helpful."

Molly started away. "I'll let her know she's going."

Beau stopped her before she got very far. "Uh-uh. I'm not the John Rolfe type. I'll deliver the message myself." When her brow lined in concern, he knew for certain that credit card fraud was the least of Jenna's worries.

"What if she turns you down?" she asked quietly.

"If she says no, you can step in and convince her. If you can't," he added grimly, "then I think you and I should have a talk about what's really going on."

TWO

"So I guess that was the young mother-to-be who was sleeping in late?"

Startled, Jenna turned quickly from closing the front door, hating the way her nerves jumped at every unexpected sound, every squeak of the hardwood flooring. If she didn't stop this, she'd make herself sick again.

She summoned a bright smile. "Yes. That was Mrs. Grant—the guest Aunt Molly mentioned when she asked you to keep the noise to a minimum."

"She didn't stay for breakfast?" Beau asked.

Jenna shook her head and smiled again. "I'm afraid she wasn't up to it—or food in general for that matter. I hope she feels better soon. She said her morning sickness lasts well into the afternoon, so that can't be a lot of fun when she's on the road. Fort Belvoir's still a long way off."

"Her husband's in the service?"

"Newly transferred," Jenna said, returning to the registration desk. Despite the frightening thoughts that had dogged her mind since that credit card call, she couldn't help noticing how good he looked. He was tall, close to six-three in his boots, and his thick sable hair was slightly long and attractively wind-tossed—just as he'd worn it as a teenager. She'd filled two diaries with thoughts about him back then—even shed a few teenage tears. But he'd been three years older and had never given her a second look. He'd been too busy entertaining prettier, curvier girls who'd been drawn to his bad boy reputation.

She tucked the bee's wax polish and cloth she'd been using back in the caddy. "So. Is there a problem in the sitting room?" She imagined there had to be since once he started a project, he rarely took a break, and he'd only arrived a short time ago.

Beau closed the distance between them, and once again, his rugged appeal made her pulse quicken. "It's a problem," he said. "But it's not work-related. I'm about to head for the diner and was wondering if you'd like to have lunch with me."

For a second, Jenna felt a burst of exhilaration. Then she remembered those funeral flowers and shook her head. She was safe here with her automatic door locks and mesh-covered windows. "Thank you," she said smiling. "But I really don't date."

"That's okay, I don't, either. And I'm not asking for a date. In fact, this would be more of an un-date."

"An un-date?" she repeated, still trying to wrap her mind around his first statement. Rumor had it that he was a bona fide dating machine who left broken hearts in his wake when he moved on.

"You've seen Disney's *Alice in Wonderland,* right?"

What did that have to do with anything? "A long time ago."

"Then you probably remember the Mad Hatter's un-birthday party. I'm asking you for an un-date. I thought having lunch would give us a few minutes to discuss the renovations, and refuel at the same time. I haven't eaten anything today." He smiled sheepishly. "Well, except for a muffin."

As if she'd been waiting in the wings for her cue, Aunt Molly breezed cheerfully into the foyer. "Did I hear someone mention the diner?"

Jenna sent her a tolerant smile. She knew a setup when she saw one. Her aunt was worried and wanted her to concentrate on something else for a while—but at the same time, wanted her to be protected. Even Courtland would think twice about hurting her if she was at Beau's side. But…

"Yes, Beau asked me to join him for lunch, but I need to strip the bed in the Blue Room and make it up for a guest who'll be coming in soon."

Aunt Molly waved off her concerns. "I can do that while you're gone. Go to lunch, and bring me back some of Aggie's wonderful Italian wedding soup." She halted abruptly, grimaced, then rebounded nicely. "That is, if that's what she's serving today. If not, any soup will do. As my Charles used to say, God rest his soul, there's nothing like soup to warm a body when the snow flies."

Jenna hid a sigh. Her darling little aunt would have never made it on the stage. This was the worst bit of acting she'd ever seen. "All right. I'll get my coat. But I'll be back in time to make up the room."

"Nonsense," Molly replied, starting up the curved staircase. "I shall do it right this minute, and I don't want to hear another word about it."

When she'd disappeared around the bend, Jenna met Beau's faintly amused expression. He was leaning casually against the high desk with his hands in his jeans pockets, and was apparently enjoying the show.

"She already phoned the diner, didn't she?"

"Yep."

"That's what I thought." Jenna released that sigh. "I'm sorry. When she gets something in her head, it takes an earthquake to dislodge it." She sent him an apologetic look. "Are you sure you want to do this?"

"Of course. I told you, the only thing I've had to eat today was—"

"Yes, I know. A muffin." She had to smile then, because in truth, she welcomed the distraction. "Thank you for humoring her. I'll see you at the diner in a few minutes."

His brow lined. "You're taking your own car?"

"Yes, I won't be staying long. Aunt Molly can handle stripping the sheets, but the beds are high and the mattresses are thick and heavy. She'll struggle making them back up. Besides, I don't want to rush you through your lunch."

"Jenna, I'll drive you back whenever you want. Believe me, I'll finish eating long before you will."

"Please," she insisted quietly. "I need to take my own car." She would've preferred to go with him— would've felt less afraid. But she couldn't go into hiding again the way she'd done after her surgery. Two years ago, panic attacks and near agoraphobia had almost eliminated what little courage she'd had left. If not for prayer, God's grace and the support of her mother and Aunt Molly, she'd be a shut-in now. She couldn't backslide—and she feared that could happen if she didn't get in her car and drive herself to the diner today.

She couldn't begin to read the thoughts moving through his eyes, but she knew he was trying to figure her out. "Okay, then," he said with a forced smile. "I'll see you at the diner."

* * *

Ten minutes later, Beau and Jenna left their vehicles in the lot and hurried through the seemingly inexhaustible flurries to the diner. The heavy wood-and-glass door closed behind them as they wiped their wet footgear on the mat. The diner was busy, three waitresses and Aggie herself delivering pots of steaming coffee and trays loaded with food. Wonderful aromas hung in the air, mingling with pop music, laughter and conversation.

Jenna felt a tingle when Beau bent to speak to her over the noise and music, his breath warm against her ear. "Booth or a table?"

"A booth," she answered. She unbuttoned her cream-colored wool coat. An echoing tingle swept through her when he touched his hand to the small of her back to guide her toward a centrally located booth. They were almost there when she saw that the back booth was empty, and made a beeline for it.

Beau assessed her curiously as she took a seat against the wall and he slid into the red vinyl booth across from her. A smile creased his rugged features.

"What's the smile about?" she asked, slipping her arms out of her coat sleeves. She smoothed her mauve sweater.

"I'm just wondering if the Mob's after you, or if you're in the witness protection program."

For just a second, she couldn't breathe. Then she realized that he was kidding and managed a laugh. She wondered how he'd react if she told him he wasn't far off. Instead of admitting that she'd wanted a clear view of the door and surrounding tables, she shrugged. "I guess I just like back booths."

"Do you also like manicotti and hot garlic bread?"

Smiling, short, stout, white-haired Aggie Benson bustled over to their booth, then flipped over their coffee mugs and filled them. "That's the special—comes with a side salad or Italian wedding soup." She nodded at the laminated menu tucked behind the chrome-and-black napkin dispenser. "But if you're looking for something that'll take a lot longer, you can always order from the menu."

Jenna smiled. "Just the wedding soup for me, Aggie, and an order of soup to go. I have to get back to the inn."

"And I'll have the works," Beau said. "Manicotti, bread, salad and—" He paused thoughtfully. "Three slices of your Dutch apple pie. Two for here, one to go. One check."

Jenna shook her head. He could pay for the pie, but— "No, we'll need two checks."

Beau sighed. "Did Alice take her own cup to the Mad Hatter's tea party?"

"No, but maybe she should have." Meeting Aggie's eyes, Jenna made a V of her fingers and spoke kindly but firmly. "Two checks, please."

Chuckling, Aggie pulled several single-serve creamers from the pocket of her black apron and dropped them on the table. "I'm not even going to ask what the Mad Hatter's tea party has to do with any of this," she said, starting away. "I'll bring your orders right out. You two can fight over the bill when the time comes."

"We'll do that," they called in unison—then shared a soft laugh.

Beau tugged a paper napkin from the dispenser and waved it like a flag of truce. "Okay. War's over. Let's talk business."

"All right. Monkey business first." Jenna stirred a

creamer and packet of sugar into her coffee. "It's fairly obvious that my aunt put you up to this lunch invitation. Why?" It took him a moment to answer, but when he did, she believed him.

"I'm not sure," he said. "I think she's worried about you, and hoped that talking to me might...I don't know...make you feel better. Does that sound right?"

Nothing would make her feel better until Courtland was behind bars, but after two years, she feared that wasn't going to happen. He was too sly, too slick and too rich. Despite Aunt Molly's suspicions, she couldn't believe the Chandlers were behind this. "Maybe."

"Would you like to talk about it?"

She shook her head. What good would that do? She'd just end up looking like a victim in his eyes. She didn't want pity from anyone, particularly the strong, confident man she found herself thinking about too often. "Sorry. I can't."

"Too personal?"

"Yes."

He studied her for a long moment, his gaze drifting over her hair and face as though committing them to memory. Then he nodded. "Okay. I'll back off. But if you change your mind, I'll be around, and I don't betray confidences."

That was good to know, she thought as Aggie crossed the dining room with their soup and salad. But there was another reason she didn't want Beau involved. She'd seen—and felt—what Courtland was capable of. He was dangerous. The fewer people taking an interest in her life, the better—for her and for them.

Talk moved to the carpeting versus hardwood issue and while they ate, Jenna opted for refinishing the hardwood. It would take longer, but in the end it would look lovely and the upkeep would be easier. That led to a discussion of other rooms and other ideas, and Beau suggested something that she'd actually considered herself.

"Your entryway is fairly large, so it wouldn't take much to create a small vestibule just inside the front door. You could add an additional door or set of doors to keep the rain and snow out of your foyer. And it would be added security for...your guests."

That got her attention. "Added security?"

He pushed his empty plate aside and dragged his coffee cup forward. "Considering the security system you've had installed and the fancy mesh covering your ground floor windows, I think you've given security a lot of thought."

"I'm...I'm responsible for the safety of my guests," Jenna replied, wondering how much Aunt Molly had told him during their take-Jenna-to-lunch conversation. She knew her aunt wouldn't betray her confidence. But Beau seemed to know that the ivy-patterned ornamental mesh she'd had installed was for her benefit, too. "What would something like that cost?"

Beau took a small notebook and pen from his back pocket.

She had the ballpark figures in her coat pocket, and they were discussing the church's upcoming bazaar over their pie and coffee when an old friend waved to her from the red Formica lunch counter at the front of the diner. Jenna waved back, and Charity's favorite octogenarian made his way past the noisy tables to their booth.

Elmer Fox was a tall, balding, walking bag of bones in a dated black-and-red plaid Woolrich jacket who couldn't have weighed more than a hundred and thirty pounds soaking wet. He carried a matching billed cap with earflaps in one hand, and a white coffee mug in the other.

Jenna moved over as the old man slid in beside her and parked his coffee on the table. "Hi, Elmer," she said. "What do you know for sure?"

He gave a low horsey laugh, his blue eyes dancing behind rimless bifocals. He included Beau in his reply. "I know it's pretty cold out and summer's a far sight away. I expect I'll be draggin' out my long johns soon."

Jenna smiled. "Think we should all pack up and move to Florida?"

Elmer chuckled. "Well, now, if we did that, there'd be no one to tend my coal fire, and you'd miss out on the nice surprise I got for you."

"You have something for me?"

"Not with me. Out at my place." He ground his back against the booth, scratching an itch. "I was lookin' through some boxes in my attic yesterday and came across some old photos. Ladies in great big bonnets, tintypes of the old Brighton Hotel before it burnt—" His rheumy blue eyes twinkled. "Even found a few of ladies in them old-fashioned bathin' suits. Hats, stockings, dresses down to their knees. I suspect them getups would get a few chuckles today."

Jenna never heard another word. Just then one of the waitresses dropped an empty tray and it waffled noisily to the floor. Instinctively, she turned in the direction of the sound—and her breath froze in her lungs when she spotted a man in a booth across from theirs who appeared to be staring at her from behind gray-tinted glasses.

Chills drizzled through her, but she couldn't look away—not even when the man in the dark parka and black watch cap turned his attention back to his news-paper.

Her rapid pulse began to slow. Okay, the man's features were similar…but the nose was all wrong, and what little hair she could see beneath his cap was too light. He wasn't Courtland. He was simply someone's visiting relative, or a tourist who'd stopped for a meal before checking out the area's huge elk herd. Maybe even a local resident she didn't recognize. Charity was small, but she didn't know everyone.

Beau reached across the table to touch her hand and she jumped.

"You okay?" he mouthed.

Jenna nodded, then flashing a smile, she shifted her attention to Elmer who had segued from a discussion of turn-of-the-century swimwear to the current trends that he just couldn't abide.

"Times were better back then. Folks could leave their doors unlocked and their keys in their cars. Now we got kids listening to rap music, walkin' all over their pant legs, gettin' tattoos and piercin' every ding dong thing the Lord gave 'em." He nodded across the room, again drawing her attention to the man in the parka. Though Jenna no longer saw him as a threat, an uneasy feeling moved through her. She watched nervously as he retrieved the cane hooked to the back of the booth, then rose, picked up his newspaper and limped toward the front register.

"It ain't just kids who've lost their minds, either," Elmer grumbled. "That goober over there's got an earring, too—saw it when he came in." He blew out a breath. "Then again, I don't expect much from a fella who can't even use his cane right."

Amused, Beau played devil's advocate. "Come on,

Elmer. We both know every generation has to do their own thing. In your day, it was spats and raccoon coats. In mine, it was Big Hair rock bands."

With a rusty laugh, Elmer levered his bony frame out of the booth. "Guess you got a point there." He shifted his gaze to Jenna. "Well, I'd best git on home. My stories will be comin' on the TV. I'll run them pictures over to you one of these days soon. I need to sort through 'em again first—divide 'em up. Maybe give some to Bertie down at the historical society."

Gathering her coat, Jenna slid out of the booth to give him a hug. "I'd love that. If you're sure you want to part with them."

"Sure as sand on the beach," he chuckled, squeezing her back. "I'll see you soon. Say hello to your aunt Molly for me." He winked. "Now there's a fine-lookin' woman."

When Elmer was out of earshot, Beau took Jenna's coat from her and held it while she slipped her arms into the sleeves. "He watches soap operas?"

"Apparently." A tiny shiver moved through her when he freed her hair from her collar. Murmuring a thank-you, she stepped away to pick up one of the checks Aggie had left, then pulled her wallet from her coat pocket.

"Please," Beau said. "Let me get that. I did invite you to lunch."

"Sorry. We've been over this. I'll pay my way, and you pay yours." She expected him to argue, but he didn't. Instead his dark eyes warmed, inexplicably making her think of sipping hot cocoa before a roaring winter fire.

"Okay. I'll get it next time."

There would be a next time?

"For now, though, we'd better pay up, grab Aunt Molly's order and make tracks before I get my walking papers. The woman I work for is a real tough cookie."

Fat flurries fell to the sidewalk and dotted Beau's navy sweatshirt as Jenna walked with him toward the lot and their respective vehicles. She knew she should be enjoying the fresh air and the thin rays of sunlight breaking through the overcast sky. Especially since she spent so much of her time indoors. But hard as she tried, she couldn't tear her eyes away from the unsettling quarter-sized depressions in the snow. Cane tracks.

"Beau?" she asked hesitantly.

He glanced down at her. "Yeah?"

"What did Elmer mean when he said the man in the parka wasn't using his cane correctly?"

He studied her for a moment, concern back in his eyes. Then he answered matter-of-factly. "The guy appeared to have a problem with his left leg, but he held his cane in his right hand. It looked strange since the point of using a cane is to take pressure off the injured limb. Why do you ask?"

Jenna worked to keep her voice from trembling. "No reason. I just wondered."

He didn't believe her. She could see it. They'd reached her white Jeep Liberty with the Blackberry's pretty floral-and-berries logo on the door. "Well," she said. "Thank you for lunch. It was nice to get out for a while." She pressed her remote and the doors unlocked. "I guess I'll see you back at the inn?"

He handed her the takeout bag, that questioning look still clouding his eyes. "I'll be there in a few minutes.

I need to check on something before I head back." He smiled. "That is, if my boss says it's okay."

"She does," Jenna replied, managing to smile back. Opening the door, she set Aunt Molly's food on the passenger's seat, then slid behind the wheel. "Now, if she was paying you by the hour, not the job, she might feel differently. But yes, take all the time you want."

"Thanks." He pulled his keys from his jeans pocket and started toward his truck. "See you soon."

"You, too," she called. Then with her smile crumbling, Jenna shut the Liberty's door, started the car and drove out of the lot. She turned onto Main Street, searching the sidewalks and shop entrances for that limping man. *Was* that Courtland behind those dark glasses? "Dear God, please, no," she whispered.

The past rushed back and she began to shake, felt her heart pound as images unfolded beyond the rhythmic slap of her windshield wipers. She saw hands like steel bands clamp her wrists—felt his hot, harsh breath on her face, saw the quick flash of the blade—

No! She would *not* let the rest of the memory come. She would *not* allow herself to become that fragile, frightened woman again. The man with the cane was simply a man with a cane, and the charges on her credit card were easily explainable mistakes.

Maybe so, a fearful voice whispered in the back of her mind. *But it's beyond coincidence when flowers are sent to three funeral homes in memory of decedents who shared your last name.*

To Jenna's right, a bubbly, middle-aged friend with a frizz of flame-red hair exited the Quick Mart, still laughing and looking back toward someone inside. A funky giraffe-head shoulder bag swung at her side. Jenna tooted her horn and waved, and always-pleasant daytime police dispatcher Sarah French waved back. Jenna swallowed hard. Since she'd returned to Charity she'd only shared her attack with three people: Aunt Molly and her two best friends. She'd felt strongly that the fewer people who knew about it, the better her chances of staying hidden. But now... Maybe it was time to speak to Sarah French's boss.

Unconcerned with the flurries that continued to toss and blow, Beau waited until Jenna's white SUV had faded from view, then cautiously walked the lot, following those cane marks in the snow. He wasn't a tracker—far from it—but he'd noticed something disturbing after Jenna mentioned the limping man. The guy's cane marks appeared consistently on the sidewalk and at the entry to the lot, but then gradually disappeared. By the time the man reached the empty space where his vehicle had been parked—a car, not a truck, from the looks of the tire tracks—the only marks in the snow were the man's footprints.

So was the cane just a walking stick, not a staff used to take pressure off a bum leg? he wondered. And if that was so, why the limp? Sympathy? Or subterfuge?

Slowly, Beau brought his hands to his hips, then looked around and exhaled raggedly, his warm breath fogging the air. This was nothing he should be getting involved in—absolutely none of his business, despite Aunt Molly's request for help. Still, he couldn't silence the thoughts running through his head. Jenna'd had the Blackberry's first floor windows covered with ornamental mesh as soon as she'd purchased the inn, and today she'd ignored the booth he'd chosen for a seat that afforded her a view of the dining room and front door. Then there was her jittery reaction to the man with the cane. When he combined those things with her current lifestyle, the only conclusion he could draw made him uneasy.

Something nasty had happened to her in Michigan. Something she feared would be repeated. But what?

What was she so afraid of?

THREE

Jenna strode inside the Blackberry, moved to the security pad behind the desk and reset the alarm as the door locked behind her. The small surveillance screen beside the key pad showed a portion of her porch and driveway, one of her first purchases when she'd bought the inn. A note from Aunt Molly lay on the desk blotter next to it. The McGraws had arrived, and taken the Rose Room. They were out now, seeing what Charity had to offer.

Setting the takeout bag on the desk and shrugging out of her coat, Jenna tried to ignore the butterflies in her stomach and called out to her aunt.

"Up here," Molly sang out. "I'm just about through."

Jenna hung her coat in the closet at the bottom of the stairs, then hurried up the steps, passing the wide landing where three tall, chalk-white Nativity figures sat on a raised platform surrounded by mini-lights and greenery. Touching a fingertip to her lips, she transferred the kiss to the infant Jesus's head, then continued on. In a moment, she'd entered the Blue Room where her great-aunt was putting the finishing touches on the queen-size bed with the hand-carved, darkly stained headboard.

The Blue Room was one of their most popular, full of romantic florals in shades of blue with layers of white sheers beneath heavy navy drapes held back with silky, braided ties. The tall armoire and mirrored dresser matched the headboard, and the ornate brass drawer pulls, crystal boudoir lamps, Oriental rugs and gilt-framed Victorian prints added another level of period romance to the room.

Molly plumped the crocheted accent pillows on the bed. "You're back early."

"But apparently, not early enough." Shaking her finger, Jenna scooped up the discarded linens from the hardwood floor. "I would've helped if you'd waited for me."

"Now, Jenny, I've been doing this for fifty years, and Lord willing, I'll be doing it for another twenty." She walked around the bed, trying to hide her concern behind a bright smile. "Now tell me about your lunch with Beau. Did you have a good time?"

"Yes, it was very nice." Her stomach lurched again as she remembered the unseen eyes behind the limping man's tinted glasses. She longed to tell her aunt about him—hear Molly say in that calm, reassuring way of hers that she was jumping at shadows again. She wanted to hear her say that she was safe now, and simply reacting to the fraudulent charges on her credit card. But Jenna loved her too much to add to her worries. In a little while, she'd call the Michigan police to see if there was any news.

"You really should go out more," her aunt chided. "Be with people your own age instead of hanging around here with an old relic like me. What did you and Beau talk about?"

"Renovations. And you're not an old relic—not according to Elmer Fox."

Molly rolled her eyes. "What's that silly old flirt saying now?"

Jenna grinned. "He thinks you're a fine-looking woman, and he's right. He found some old photographs and tintypes in his attic and said we can look through them if we want."

Jenna carried the sheets through the doorway to the laundry chute in the hall. Years ago it had been a dumbwaiter, but now served to escort clothes and bedding to the basement's laundry room. If she thought bringing up Elmer would derail her aunt's interest in her lunch with Beau, she was wrong.

"You couldn't have talked about renovations the whole time," Molly persisted, following. "Did he mention if he was seeing anyone right now? And by seeing, I mean—"

"I know what 'seeing' means," Jenna returned. "And no, he didn't."

"Well, this is just my opinion, but you could do a lot worse than that young man. He goes to church, he's got a thriving business, and he's not half bad to look at."

No, he wasn't. But she wasn't looking for someone who'd always be looking for someone else. "Trying to get rid of me, Aunt Molly?"

"Of course not, but it's time you thought about settling down with a good man."

The doorbell rang as Jenna unlatched the spring-loaded cream-and-pink door that matched the striped wallpaper, and she quickly tossed the sheets inside. "I'll get that," she said, glad to end the conversation. "My turn to do some work around here."

She didn't have to check the monitor to see who

was on the porch. A peculiar-looking woman peered through the wide, etched-glass side light to the left of the front door, her gloved hands clutching the sides of her bulky gray corduroy jacket together. Beau's idea to divide the long foyer into a vestibule and entry gained more merit. The temperature outside was only in the low forties, but the poor woman looked frozen.

Ignoring the button behind the desk, she hurried to the door to manually unlock it. "Good afternoon," she said, smiling and holding the door open. The woman with the bouffant hair style and big round glasses rushed inside as though she'd never experienced snow, and Jenna closed the door. For a second she was startled by the windblown brown cowlick on the crown of the woman's head, then realized that she was wearing a synthetic wig. "You must be Mrs. Bolton."

"Guilty as charged," she laughed, reaching up to smooth her "hair." "And you must be Jenna. I recognize your voice from our phone conversation. Goodness, it's cold up here." Without waiting for Jenna to reply, she continued into the foyer, her head swiveling as she took in the high ceiling, cream-and-pink wallpaper, huge silk flower wreaths and swags, and wistful window treatments. The Victorian age had been all about excess, and Aunt Molly had decorated the foyer—the entire inn, for that matter—with that in mind. To the right, a curved wall held built-in shelves filled with pretty jars of jam, fragrant candles and assorted candies, figurines and lace doilies.

"How absolutely lovely," Audrey Bolton said. "I can't wait to see the rest of the inn."

"And we can't wait to show it off," Aunt Molly called, smiling as she descended the stairs in her Victorian trappings. "Welcome to the Blackberry." She offered her hand to the woman. "I'm Molly Jennings, prior owner and current hanger-on. The inn belongs to my niece now."

Bolton put down her bag, then slipped off a glove to clasp it, her features telegraphing her delight at Molly's period dress.

"When you've registered," Molly went on, "I'll show you to your room and give you the tour. In the meantime, I'll freshen the coffee on the dining room buffet, and add a few pastries. We like to leave a little something out for our guests."

"Wonderful." Beaming, the woman walked with Jenna to the desk. "I can't tell you how glad I am to have found your listing in the phone book." She slid the long strap of her purse off her shoulder, then reached inside for her wallet. "I usually stay in hotels when I do an audit. This is my first stay at a bed and breakfast."

"Well, we certainly hope it won't be your last." Jenna slid a card and pen across the desk and pulled up Mrs. Bolton's registration on the computer. "Let's see... You gave me most of your information over the phone. You'll be with us for two nights, correct?"

"That's right."

"Great. Then I'll just need your driver's license, credit card and signature." No wonder she was chilled to the bone, Jenna thought, reading the woman's home address on the screen. She'd forgotten that Audrey Bolton hailed from North Carolina.

"About my credit card," Bolton said, producing her credentials, then signing the card and sliding it back across the desktop. "I'm one of those dinosaurs who doesn't care to use plastic. I think it's the bane of civilization, with people using it indiscriminately and getting themselves in all sorts of trouble. I only have a card because some hotels insist upon two forms of identification, and I travel a lot. So if you don't mind, I'd prefer to pay cash."

Jenna understood perfectly. "Cash works for me." She didn't think credit cards were the bane of civilization, but she couldn't deny wishing she'd cancelled hers before someone hacked into her account. "I'm afraid we do need to have a credit card on file to cover any additional charges." She turned the computer screen toward her guest. "But when you're ready to check out, I can delete the card number you used to reserve the room."

"Thank you. I'd appreciate that." Easing close to the monitor, she appeared to check the room charge, then tucked her credentials back into her wallet and removed several bills. "If it's okay, I'd like to settle up in advance. I won't be making any long distance calls while I'm here, and if I decide I need a jar or two of your lovely jams, I'll pay for them with cash."

"Sounds good," Jenna said, but she was suddenly feeling a little distrustful. Maybe it was the wig, or the cash thing. Or the wig *and* the cash thing. Or maybe her suspicion was based on her own paranoia. She shook off those thoughts. She had no choice but to trust the woman. She couldn't run an inn and doubt every guest who walked through the door.

"Here you go," she said, handing Mrs. Bolton her room key. "You're in the Blue Room. Aunt Molly will be back in a minute to show you the way, but it's the second door on the left at the top of the stairs. If you have a problem after lights out, just give me a call." She nodded toward the wide archway leading to the turquoise-and-gold parlor and the hallway beyond. "If there's anything you need, my room's at the end of the hall, and my number's on the nightstand in your room.

Oh—and if you go out and need to get back in, you'll need to tap today's code into the security pad located next to the side door. It's one-forty-two plus your room number—three."

"One-four-two-three," she said. "Got it." Then she smiled at the brass key in her open hand. "I thought these things were extinct. No plastic key card with a magnetic strip? With the exception of the security pad, I feel like I've fallen into a time warp."

Jenna laughed softly. "I don't know about that, but you'll find we're pretty laid back around here."

"Great." The woman wearing the dangling peace sign earrings gave Jenna another bright smile. "'Laid back' is exactly what I was hoping for."

Beau opened a can of soup, dumped it in a saucepan, and turned on the burner beneath it. He'd stayed at the Blackberry until after six this evening to make up for the time he'd lost, but with guests in three of Jenna's rooms, he'd had to keep the noise down. The work he'd planned to accomplish today would have to wait until tomorrow. Then again, maybe making up the work had nothing to do with his staying late. Maybe he'd hung around in case Jenna wanted to talk. He stirred the soup…couldn't get her out of his mind. Couldn't get the guy with the cane out of his mind, either.

Two sharp reports broke the stillness of his kitchen, and Beau whirled from the range—froze—then turned off the soup and grabbed a jacket and flashlight. He rushed outside.

The night was cold and clear after the daylong flurries, and every star in the heavens twinkled in a black, moonless sky. Quickly, he checked the perimeter of his house and the inside of his garage, then sprinted across the dusting of snow behind the garage to his carpentry shop. In a second, he'd unlocked the door and reached around the corner to flick on the overhead track lights. Long bright tubes illuminated every corner of the forty-by-forty foot space.

Inhaling the pleasant smell of cut wood, he stepped inside, then took a slow walk over a concrete floor lightly coated with sawdust. Nothing seemed to have been disturbed. Not the stacks of lumber against the wall, or the oak cabinets draped in clear plastic that awaited a coat of stain. Not the neatly piled rolls of insulation left over from his last job. He crossed the floor to his line of power tools. No problem there, either... and all of his hand tools hung just as he'd left them on the peg board above his long work bench. Both windows were tightly locked.

So what had he heard? Gunshots? Kids outlawing deer? A car backfiring? All three were possibilities since he lived in the boonies where no one could complain about the irritating ring of power tools or his lousy singing voice.

He stood there for another long moment. Then he locked the shop and returned to the house he'd purchased last year, scanning the woods around him as he walked. But nothing moved in the pines and leafless trees, and in a minute he was stirring soup again.

He liked his one-story ranch house. It wasn't a showplace like Jenna's—not yet. But it suited him, it was paid for, and as soon as he finished the Blackberry's renovations, he'd be tearing down walls, ripping up flooring, and eventually making this the home he'd longed for since he was a kid. It wasn't much, but it had potential and it was miles from the shack on the other side of the railroad tracks where he'd grown up.

For the first eighteen years of his life, he'd lived—
or maybe *existed* was the better word—in one of the
old tannery row houses that were still standing at the
time. Theirs was a dilapidated wood-frame with peel-
ing paint that should've been condemned long before
it was torn down.

He stopped stirring for a moment.

Funny how one thought spawned another, like a flat
stone skipping across a pond. He hadn't thought of that
place in years, and now every nail hole in the walls—
every cracked section of linoleum—seemed to sharpen
in his mind as he recalled one of his first memories in
that house. It was a memory he'd never shared with
anyone. He was a three-year-old watching his mother
walk out the door thinking—wrongly—that she'd be
coming back. He had no memory of his father, had
no idea who he was and had no interest in looking for
him—or his mother.

The only family he'd ever known was the grandfather who'd raised him out of duty, and there'd been
nothing grand about him. Considering the late Jasper
Travis's cold, unyielding nature, he didn't blame his
mother for skipping out. He only blamed her for not
taking him with her.

Beau took the soup off the stove, dumped it in a
bowl and carried it to the department-store table that
had come with the house, his thoughts rolling on. His
life was different now. Military service, trade school
and a dozen years of decent living had blunted his old
reputation. But to some, he would always be that wild
Welfare kid from tannery row. Small towns had long
memories. People still talked about the spree he and
his friends had gone on one night years ago, raiding
gardens and painting the headlights of a dozen cars

black. The owners of the vehicles had gone ballistic—demanded that they all be jailed on the spot or shipped off to juvvie. And for a while there, it looked like the district magistrate would do it.

Thank God for Molly Jennings. When Jasper refused to pay his fines and sneered that juvenile detention was the best place for him, like a skinny angel in high button shoes, she'd marched inside the magistrate's office and told Jasper that *wasn't* going to happen.

Beau smiled. He still wasn't sure if she'd saved his skin out of Christian duty, or if she'd just decided that he needed straightening out and she was the woman for the job. She'd made him an offer that day. She'd pay his fines and his share of restitution to the owners under two conditions. He was to work off his debt doing odd jobs for her, and he was to start attending church regularly.

He was a better man today because of Aunt Molly.

Beau slid the box of saltines closer, opened one of the wrapped stacks, and crushed a few crackers into his chicken noodle soup. There was nothing he wouldn't do for his skinny little benefactor. And as of today, that meant watching over the niece she loved like a daughter. He'd do it for her…and for Jenna. Because like it or not, his old feelings for her were coming back.

He just wished he knew what or whom he was supposed to protect her from.

At seven-forty-seven that night, he stood before the bathroom mirror in his Pittsburgh hotel room, staring at his clean-shaven reflection and newly colored hair. Smiling, he fashioned it into a short ponytail at the back of his head. He was beginning to enjoy this masquerade.

Wandering into the nearly dark bedroom, he poured wine into the glass tumbler beside the ice bucket, then walked to the long plate-glass window to consider the Pittsburgh skyline. The city at night was stunning, millions of lights shining in the darkness from every soaring skyscraper to the lowliest shop...outlining the bridge on the Monongahela River and the ships moving beneath it. It was a far cry from where he'd been this morning.

He sipped and savored, his thoughts rolling on until those he didn't want to contemplate intruded, and the wine turned to vinegar in his mouth.

Whirling away from the Golden Triangle's bright lights, he strode to the nightstand, clicked on a lamp and picked up his disposable cell phone. He speed-dialed the employees he'd met earlier at The Tall Spruce Travel Lodge—two shadowy forces who came highly recommended, and would do as he asked without blinking an eye because the money was good, and that was how they made their living. He waited through nearly a dozen rings, then impatiently disconnected and dialed again. This time, the tall one with the shaved head and muscular physique answered on his own disposable phone.

"What took you so long?" he snapped coldly.

"I was indisposed."

How he hated smart-mouthed thugs. "I'm paying you to be available to me 24-7. That's your only priority. Did your partner accomplish his task this evening?"

"He did. The subject left his home to investigate. He didn't appear to find anything."

"Good." When—or if—the bullet holes were discovered, the shots fired into the sign on Travis's shop would be blamed on vandals, barely investigated and quickly forgotten. He knew the immaturity of the act was beneath him. But making Travis scramble gave him an enormous sense of satisfaction for several reasons—not the least of which was the fact that she liked him. "Let me know when the woman contacts you."

"I will."

Pushing the disconnect button, he returned the phone to the nightstand, his thoughts shifting, hatred heating his blood. After watching the inn for the past week without catching a glimpse of her, he'd been startled to see her at that little diner today. It had taken every ounce of his willpower to stay away from her, to stay calm. But it was important that he remained hidden. He wanted to strip her of everything that gave her pleasure before he faced her. Every last thing. Then…then when the time was right, when her fears were at their peak and her life was in shambles, they'd have a short, sweet talk about consequences.

Then he'd kill her.

FOUR

Outside, night wrapped the Blackberry in a quiet cocoon, pressing against the windows and doors…keeping goodness in and evil out? Jenna flicked a glance at the grandfather clock in the foyer, saw that it was a few minutes before nine, then leafed through her Rolodex for the Michigan number she'd called earlier. A minute later, she'd identified herself to the secretary, and the woman had put her through to the lead investigator in her case.

The instant she heard Detective Sergeant Ray Caspian's out-of-breath baritone, Jenna regretted calling; she'd apparently phoned at a bad time. She was surprised when the olive-skinned, slightly overweight officer offered his own apology.

"Ms. Harper, this is Ray Caspian. Forgive me for not getting back to you earlier. I'm afraid I inherited some chaos when I came in at four. But I did get the message that you wanted to speak with me."

"There's no need to apologize, Detective. But yes, if you have a few minutes, I did have a question. I imagine you know what it is."

"Yes. And actually, when I heard you'd phoned, I made a few calls." He gentled his voice. "Now, obviously your case is still open, but it's been two years, and unfortunately current cases get more attention. Unless someone comes forward with new information, we have to center our efforts on other crimes. I'm truly sorry, but out of necessity, your case has been back-burnered."

Jenna's spirits sank, but she pressed on. "So these phone calls you made... I guess none of Courtland's friends or associates have heard from him."

"No ma'am, and I get the sense that if they had heard something, they would've let us know. I don't believe the guy was well liked."

Based on what she'd seen, she had to agree—which should've been an immediate tip-off to her that there was something not quite right about him. He'd barely mentioned friends and family, and when they'd gone out, usually to the theatre or a trendy restaurant, the people he'd spoken with were business associates. None of them had returned his greeting with anything approaching warmth. Four dates. They'd had four dates. And she hadn't seen who he was until he began to— She drew a breath and shook off the memory.

"Well, thank you for looking into this again," she murmured, trying to hide her disappointment. "I just— Well, he's been on my mind lately, and I was hoping that he'd surfaced somewhere and you'd heard about it."

Her reply seemed to sharpen Caspian's interest, though nothing changed in his understanding tone. "Believe me, Ms. Harper, if we'd heard something, I would've notified you personally. Can I ask why he's been on your mind? Did something happen? Or is it just the two-year anniversary that prompted you to call?"

Jenna stilled as gooseflesh covered her skin. *November seventeenth. Four days from now.* She hadn't thought about it consciously. But...*was* it the two-year anniversary that brought back the clawing fear? Had the date been simmering in her unconscious mind for a while, just waiting for something out of the ordinary to bring it to the fore? Something like identity theft or a stranger with a limp?

"Ma'am?" he prodded. "Is there something you want to tell me?"

For just a second, she nearly said yes. But he was busy, his jurisdiction was miles away and suddenly she realized she might have jumped to some incorrect conclusions. "No. No, there's nothing. Thank you for making those calls. I hope I didn't pull you away from your work at a bad time."

He didn't say she had or hadn't. He simply told her to call him anytime. He wanted to see the case resolved as badly as she did. Then they wished each other a good night, and Jenna hung up. She was standing behind the desk with her hand still on the cordless handset when her great-aunt came quietly into the foyer—no mean feat wearing clunky high button shoes.

"You called Detective Caspian."

Jenna smiled wanly. She'd wanted to make the call secretly to minimize her aunt's concern. Obviously, she'd failed. "Reading my mind?"

"No, I'm afraid I was eavesdropping on the way to my room."

Her "room" was actually a small, pretty suite on the second floor, complete with a sitting room, bath and tiny kitchenette. Jenna had pleaded with her several times to move to the first floor so she didn't have to use the stairs so often. But Molly wouldn't leave the quarters she'd shared with her late husband.

"I take it there's no news," Molly went on.

"Unfortunately, no. But as they say—whoever 'they'

are—no news is good news." Jenna walked around the desk. "Detective Caspian assured me that if the status of the case changes, he'll call me."

"As he should. In the meantime, we'll keep praying that the police find that horrid man and lock him up." Sighing then, she changed the subject. "I filled both coffeemakers and set the timers, and the table's ready. The McGraws and their granddaughter will be leaving early, so they'd like to have breakfast at seven-thirty, and Mrs. Jackson will join them." She frowned. "Mrs. Bolton said she prefers to skip breakfast."

"Yes, I know. She wants to sleep in since she only has to leave for her audit around eleven. I offered to fix her a late breakfast, but she insisted that coffee and a bagel is all she usually has in the morning—if that. I'll offer her something again when she comes downstairs."

"Very good. All of our ducks are in a row. Did she say who she's auditing? One of the businesses?"

That stopped Jenna for a moment. "I don't know. She didn't mention it. The information's probably confidential anyway."

"Probably." Molly eased up on tiptoe for a hug. "And now that our guests are tucked in for the night, I believe I'll scoot up to my little nest, brew a nice cup of tea, and do some reading before I close my eyes. I'll see you at six-fifteen."

Jenna shook her head. "No, stay in bed for a while. Get a good night's sleep. I've already made the pie shells for the Quiche Lorraine so most of the prep work's finished."

Molly chuckled softly. "You talked me right into it. I'll see you at seven." She'd nearly made it to the curve in the staircase when she turned around. "Have you given any more thought to the self-defense classes Rachel mentioned last week?"

Actually she had, but until today, she'd decided against it.

"Do it," Molly said. "It would be good for you. You girls should spend more time together." Before Jenna could remind her diminutive aunt that attending classes meant leaving the inn unattended, she added, "I don't know how long classes run, but business is always slow in the winter, and if we have guests, I'm perfectly capable of holding the fort for a few hours."

Jenna blew her a kiss. "I'll think about it. Sleep tight, Aunt Molly."

"You, too. And don't worry. I'll be having a talk with the Lord tonight. He'll see us safely through to morning."

"I know He will," Jenna murmured. "Good night."

"Good night, dear."

Jenna watched her disappear, then double checked the doors and security panel, made certain the exterior lights were still throwing a radiant halo around the inn, then dimmed the chandelier in the foyer and one of the parlor's Tiffany lamps. Despite her nightly routine, she felt slightly better about the events of the day after speaking with Detective Caspian.

No news *was* good news.

Jenna's rooms were smaller than Molly's, but like several of the Blackberry's fussy bedchambers, her dusty-peach-and-cream quarters had a small bath and sitting room. She'd just taken her Bible from her nightstand, when her personal line rang. She recognized the low masculine voice on the phone instantly, and a few happy butterflies took flight in her stomach.

"Jenna, it's Beau Travis. I hope it's not too late to call."

"Not at all," she returned. "What can I do for you?"

He laughed softly. "Actually, I was hoping I could do something for you."

"Oh? What?"

"Make you feel better about what happened this morning. It's kind of a misery-loves-company thing. There's a news magazine show on TV right now doing a story on how widespread identity theft is. It's nearly over, but you can still catch the last few minutes. When they come back from the break, they'll be talking about ways to prevent it."

She had a small flat-screen television set in her room, but there was nothing to gain from watching the program because she had no intention of getting another credit card. "Thanks, but I think I heard every tip imaginable from the rep who phoned this morning. She was very thorough."

"Right. I didn't think of that. I just thought… Well, that this was information you should probably have."

He drew a breath—one of those deep intakes of air that usually signaled a caller was about to sign off. Then he didn't.

"If you belong to any social networks, they're going to discuss ways to discourage hackers from messing with those, too. That might be helpful for your business."

Jenna smiled against the receiver, not only because he'd called, but because he seemed to want to stay on the line. "Thanks, but I don't belong to any of them. Most of our guests are repeat customers or people who've heard about us through word of mouth." Despite all the assurances they touted, even Facebook's creator had been hacked, so no one's security was a hundred percent dependable. Social networks were for people who wanted to share. Not for those who wanted to remain hidden. "We don't even have a webpage."

"No? Then you're hacker proof. In that area, anyhow."

"I just don't understand why men do such idiotic things."

"The same reason they create computer viruses. Because they can." He paused, and when he spoke again, there was a smile in his voice. "And who says they're all men?"

"They have to be. No woman would do something like that."

Laughter rustled in Beau's throat, and Jenna warmed to the sound of it. "Anyway, as long as we're talking... Thank you again for humoring my aunt this morning. I hadn't been out to lunch in a while, and it felt good."

"Did it?"

The question surprised her. "Well...yes."

"Good. I only asked because toward the end, you seemed uneasy. And to be honest, that's really why I called tonight. I was concerned about you."

It had been a long time since a man had expressed concern for her. A very long time. Somewhere in the back of her mind, she wanted to explain—about the flowers, about the limping man, about the assault that had nearly taken her life. But she couldn't do it. "I'm fine," she said quietly, "but thank you for that."

"You're welcome. Now I'll say good night and let you get some sleep."

"Good night. I'll see you in the morning."

"Yep, see you then."

Jenna hung up, then slowly eased back against her

pillows again. Talking with Beau had been nice, and talking with Detective Caspian had been encouraging. But Beau's mentioning her uneasiness opened a cold spot of fear in her chest. Needing their joyful reassurance, she opened her Bible to the Psalms. She'd read many of them so often that the pages were worn and she could quote the verses, verbatim. Especially Psalm 23. But tonight, she turned the page to Psalm 27:1.

"The Lord is my light and my salvation—whom shall I fear? The Lord is the stronghold of my life. Of whom shall I be afraid?" She continued to read, eventually coming to a verse that gave her the most comfort. *"In times of trouble He will shelter me; He will keep me safe in His Temple and make me secure on a high rock."*

"No one," she whispered, thinking of the first verse again. "I shouldn't fear anyone, Lord, because I know that I'm not leaving this world for the next until You say it's time." She swallowed a sudden lump in her throat. "But if it's Your will, I'd like to stay for a while. I love it here with my friends and family. Please bless them and keep them safe. Keep us all safe."

Gentling her voice then, she put the Bible on the nightstand and turned off the lamp to finish her prayers in the darkness. She felt more connected to her Creator without the distractions of light and color.

"I've thanked You many times for the gifts You've given me," she murmured. "Especially the gift of life after the attack. But forgive me, in some ways I feel empty. I don't mean to be envious of my friends, but You've given Rachel and Margo good men to love, and some days I feel short changed because I can't let anyone into my life when there's a man out there who might want to finish what he started two years ago. So please… If it's Your will that I have a loving home and family some day, help Detective Caspian find him, and put him in a place where he can't hurt anyone ever again.

"One more thing," she whispered. "There's a new friend I'd like to remember in my prayers. I suspect You already know and like him. He's a good man, Father—a carpenter like your Son, Jesus. Please bless him, too."

Night passed swiftly, and at 6:00 a.m. on Friday morning, Jenna awoke from a deep sleep, thoroughly rested and surprisingly calm. Silencing her alarm clock, she quickly showered and dressed in a white T-shirt and powder-blue fleece tracksuit. She was in the dimly lit kitchen twenty minutes later. Turning on the light over the butcher-block work island, she gathered Swiss cheese, eggs, cream and crumbled bacon, and started the quiche.

When the pie shells were filled and in the oven, she pulled out the recipe for the caramel latte crunch cups she'd received from her friend Richard, a fellow bed-and-breakfast owner who hailed from New York.

She'd just flicked on the light over the sink and started to gather the ingredients when she spotted a moving speck. Startled, she grabbed a napkin from the holder nearby and squashed it. She released a soft cry when another one scurried out from behind the row of clear glass canisters on the countertop. Chills peppering her arms now, Jenna reached out to slowly move the canister away from the wall. And recoiled!

Ants! Dozens of them, racing and scurrying over the spilled sugar behind the canisters—crawling along the wall, marching upward toward the oak cupboards!

Dear God, where had they come from? The Blackberry didn't *have* an ant problem—had never had a pest problem of any kind!

Grabbing more napkins, she fought her revulsion and dispatched those she could see, then quickly strode to the broom closet off the kitchen for the vacuum cleaner. Minutes later, the ants and spilled sugar were gone, the floor was vacuumed, and the sweeper bag was stuffed inside a plastic bag and tossed outside.

Shuddering, rubbing the goose bumps on her arms, she went back inside to disinfect the countertop. Then she checked the seals on the canisters and searched every drawer and cupboard. The ants appeared to be gone, but that didn't calm her rattled nerves. She knew there could be more lurking, unseen. But she didn't have the luxury of continuing her search. The clock was ticking; she had to start breakfast for her guests.

"Please, God," she prayed shakily. "I won't ask for another thing this week if You'll just keep them off the dining room table."

Abandoning the crunch cups that would take too long to prepare, she pulled frozen blueberries from the freezer, threw together her favorite muffin recipe, then added a streusel topping and slid them into the oven.

She'd just found a classical music station on the radio when Aunt Molly came into the kitchen. The dread on Jenna's face stopped her cheery "Good morning" before both words were out.

"What's wrong?"

Jenna shook her head. Now wasn't the time to discuss what an ant infestation could do to their business—especially when she was battling time. "Tell you later. The McGraws will be coming downstairs in a few minutes." She nodded toward the small footed crystal bowls on the countertop and tried to keep her voice from trembling. "For now, could you fill the juice and milk carafes while I wash and load the fruit bowls?"

"Of course, dear," she replied uneasily. She didn't press Jenna for an explanation or ask why her niece had opened new bags of flour and sugar when there were filled canisters on the counter. She didn't ask why Jenna had to wash perfectly clean bowls. She simply went to the refrigerator in a rustle of burgundy taffeta and lace, and got to work.

"Ants?" Molly whispered as she and Jenna watched their smiling guests through the kitchen's pass-through window to the dining room. Six-year-old Matilda "Mattie" McGraw had been regaling her graying grandparents and middle-aged sales rep Sylvia Price with riddles ever since they'd sat down, and the mood in the dining room was warm and festive.

"The Blackberry has *never* had ants," Molly went on nervously. "We must call someone. Preferably someone who'll be discreet. I shudder to think of a van with a big ugly bug on the roof parked outside the inn for the world to see."

Jenna couldn't agree more. It was no sin if a few of God's less desirable creatures found their way into a clean home, but that philosophy changed when it came to running a business where food was served. Gossip thrived in Charity like kudzu in the south. "There's someone in town," she replied, keeping her voice low. "I'll call as soon as he opens."

"Good," Aunt Molly whispered. "Please ask him to park in back and use the kitchen entrance—if possible, after our guests have gone."

Nodding, Jenna met her aunt's eyes, then reluctantly brought up something she'd wondered about for the past hour. It was difficult to ask the question without hinting at blame, but she had to know. "Aunt Molly, forgive me, but when you set the table and coffeemaker for breakfast last night, did you happen to fill the sugar bowl, too?"

"No," she returned quietly, "it was already full, and if I'd spilled sugar, I would have cleaned it up." When Jenna winced, she rushed to put her at ease. "I'm not offended. You had to ask."

Yes, she did. But Molly's answer brought disturbing thoughts to the surface again. Even if one of her guests had wandered into the kitchen last night for a snack or a beverage, there was no reason for anyone to touch the sugar canister. If they'd wanted coffee or tea, the buffet in the dining room held carafes and plenty of condiments.

On the other side of the pass-through window, Mr. McGraw had drained his coffee cup and was glancing around. Grabbing the decaf pot from the coffeemaker, Jenna went into the dining room where the little comedian with the long silky bangs and waist-length strawberry-blond hair had just offered up another riddle. She was a darling little thing in a fuzzy pink sweater, and she seemed to have an incurable case of the giggles. The sprinkling of freckles across her nose belonged to her alone, but her green eyes had come from her grandfather.

Grinning, Max McGraw thanked Jenna for the refill, then turned to his granddaughter. "Maybe you should ask Ms. Harper that one. She *has* to be better at this than Grammy and I are."

"Okay," Mattie said, giggling. "How do you get an elephant in a matchbox?"

Jenna had to laugh. How secure the very young

were. She could use a big helping of that today. "I don't know, Mattie. How do you get an elephant in a match box?"

"You dump out the matches. How do you get a tyrannosaurus rex in a match box?"

Thoroughly enchanted now, Jenna guessed, "Dump out the matches?"

"No," she said, full of giggles again. "Dump out the elephant."

What a wonderful way to start the day, Jenna thought a few minutes later as she carried the coffeepot back into the kitchen: sharing breakfast and laughing with a child. But as that thought gained strength, her warm mood evaporated. Because children were a gift she might never have. And that was so much worse than finding ants in her kitchen.

By nine-forty-five, the McGraws and Ms. Price were on their way, and Jenna had spoken to Jim Gannon of Surefire Pest Control. He'd agreed to come by around ten-fifteen. The next thirty minutes couldn't pass quickly enough.

Visibly distressed, Molly reentered the kitchen, fresh from her second trip to the top of the stairs. "There isn't a sound up there," she said. "No rattling water pipes, no TV. If Mrs. Bolton doesn't come down soon, she won't even have time for a bagel before she leaves for her audit." She fiddled nervously with the cameo at her throat. "What if she's ill?"

Jenna hesitated for several moments, during which her great-aunt's questioning gaze remained on hers. She hated to wake a guest who wanted to sleep, but Molly had a point. Three points, actually. She wanted their guests to be well, and she wanted them to enjoy the full hospitality of the Blackberry. But she was also adverse to someone showing up with a wand and a pesticide canister while a guest was enjoying her morning coffee in the next room. "I'll tap at her door. Maybe she forgot to set the alarm clock, or shut it off and fell back to—"

A pitiful groan issued from Aunt Molly's throat when a quick series of raps sounded at the kitchen door. Jenna sighed. It wasn't Beau; he always came to the front door.

The bug man was here.

Fifteen minutes later, Gannon stared curiously at the nearly half-inch long, reddish-brown ants he'd removed from Jenna's vacuum cleaner bag and placed in the empty jar she'd supplied—three skittering little cretins that made Jenna's skin crawl. Turning it this way and that, Gannon watched them scale the inside of the glass jar.

He was a short man somewhere between thirty and forty with a slight build, hazel eyes, thinning brown hair and a nice smile. His denim jacket has seen better days. After another moment, he turned to Jenna. Aunt Molly was in the foyer, guarding the desk and preparing to steer Mrs. Bolton away from the kitchen door if she came downstairs.

"Okay, I'm stumped," he said.

"Stumped?"

"Yeah. I've only been doing this for a couple of years, but I'm very familiar with the types of ants we have in the area. Pavement ants are the culprits that generally invade houses. They're the little buggers that make small mounds of sand near sidewalks, driveways and the sides of houses. We also have carpenter ants, pharaoh ants and thief ants in the area. But these guys—these guys are different. I'll need to do some research."

"Research?" Jenna repeated, startled. She didn't want him to research the ants, she wanted him to terminate them. Right now.

"Yeah, I can't get rid of them if I don't know what they're all about. Different species prefer different foods, and react to different treatments." He turned to leave, speaking over his shoulder. "Don't worry, I'll get back to you soon—hopefully within the hour."

Jenna followed him to the door, her mind alive with questions. "Mr. Gannon, wait. Isn't it unusual to see ants in the winter?"

"Not if they're living in the walls," he said, and another chill moved through her. "It *is* unusual to see them during the winter in a home that's never had an ant problem before, though." Sending her a reassuring smile, he tilted the jelly jar. "I want to do this right. As soon as I find out who these guys are, I'll be back and we'll decide on a plan of attack."

When he'd gone, Molly came into the kitchen. "What did he say?"

Jenna sighed. "Apparently we have alien ants. He left to do some research on the best way to get rid of them. Mrs. Bolton hasn't stirred yet?"

"No. And it's getting late."

Jenna glanced at the kitchen clock. "Okay, I'll go check on her."

"And I'll get the phone," Molly said as it began to ring.

A minute later, Jenna knocked softly at the Blue Room's door, then listened for the reply that didn't come. She knocked again, louder this time. "Mrs.

Bolton? Are you up?" But again, nothing stirred beyond the door.

Now she was beginning to worry. Was the woman a deep sleeper? Or was she sick and in need of help?

Quickly returning to the foyer, Jenna retrieved the master key and rushed back upstairs. She unlocked the door—opened it a crack. "Mrs. Bolton?"

Cool morning light filtered through a narrow space between the drawn drapes, laying a thin ribbon of sunlight across the Blue Room's perfectly made, silky-smooth, quilted floral comforter. And a feeling of dread settled over her.

The bed hadn't been slept in.

Rushing inside, Jenna yanked open the drapes, flooding the room with sunshine. She took a disbelieving glance around, then checked the closet and armoire—opened the bureau drawers. Empty! She enlarged her search. There wasn't a thing out of place. Not a tissue in the wastebasket, a hair in the bathroom sink, or a wrinkle in the quilted shams or accent pillows stacked against the carved headboard.

She strode to the window, pulled back the sheers and looked down at the empty parking space in the Blackberry's small lot. Audrey Bolton was gone.

Then movement caught her eye, and Jenna's heart fell as she watched a half dozen moving specks skitter over the windowsill and scale the wood frames.

Dear God in Heaven. They were up here, too.

FIVE

Beau and Aunt Molly were deep in discussion when Jenna came downstairs a minute later, and from the somber look on his face, her aunt had just told him how their morning had gone.

"Sorry about the ants," he said when she'd reached the last step.

"Thanks. Me, too." She stepped down to the floor. "I'm even sorrier that we're missing a guest."

Molly stared incredulously. "She's not up there?"

"No. She's gone, and there are ants in the Blue Room, too. I killed at least a dozen."

Molly's parchment complexion seemed to pale even more. "I just booked that room."

"Then we're going to have to un-book it."

"Hang on a minute," Beau said, his brow creasing. As always, he wore jeans and boots. A gray sweatshirt showed beneath his open brown bomber jacket. "I don't get this ant thing. I just repaired a wall in that room. If the ants had been there last week, I would've seen them."

Jenna answered wearily. "Apparently they're just making their way up from the kitchen. Aunt Molly, when did your guest want to arrive?"

"Tomorrow evening. They planned to stay for three days. But I fear that's not going to work now."

Jenna shook her head. This just didn't make any sense. Aunt Molly hadn't mentioned finding ants in her quarters, and she kept a small amount of food upstairs. Why would there be ants in a room that was food free, except for the occasional snack brought in by her guests? Also, if Mrs. Bolton had seen ants, it seemed as though someone as frank as she'd been would've said something. That reasoning also seemed to apply if she'd had an emergency or received a cell phone call that took her away. Audrey Bolton would have left a note.

The phone rang again. Hoping the caller was their missing guest, Jenna moved behind the desk to pick up the receiver. She was surprised when Jim Gannon identified himself. He'd only been gone ten or fifteen minutes.

"Ms. Harper, have you had children staying with you recently?"

She cocked her head, thinking it a strange question. "As a matter of fact, yes. She left this morning with her grandparents."

"That could explain your problem, then. The ants you found are called red harvesters. They're mostly found in the plains of west Texas, and they don't invade homes or gravitate toward sugar. They're seed gatherers."

Seed gatherers? Jenna's mind spun. "I—I don't understand. If they're primarily found on the Texas plains and they don't invade homes, how did they get here?"

"I was puzzled by that, too, until I read that harvesters are generally sold for ant farms. I doubt you have a colony, Ms. Harper. I think some of them went AWOL. Any chance the little girl you mentioned could have—"

"Brought an ant farm inside and allowed a few of them to escape?" Her fear, still so close to the surface, began to build. "No, this little girl was a sweet six-year-old, and her grandparents were good people. If anything like that had happened, they would have let me know about it. Even if it was an accident."

"You're certain?"

"As certain as I can be."

"Then I'm sorry, but I think somebody's messing with you. I'll fix you up with some ant traps. That should take care of the remaining troublemakers. In the meantime, if you have borax on hand—"

The rest of his words barely registered as Jenna's scalp began to prickle. Clamping the phone between her cheek and shoulder, she quickly called up a file on her computer. A few seconds later, she was staring at an empty screen. All of Audrey Bolton's information— her name, address, credit card number and room assignment—had vanished along with her. Heart pounding, she met the sober question in Beau's eyes. Her computer was password protected, and there was no way she'd left it on last night before she went to bed.

Murmuring her thanks to Gannon, she said goodbye, hung up and moved to the front of the desk to speak to her great-aunt. She'd obviously been following Jenna's side of the conversation and the distress in her eyes said she'd made the correct assumptions. "Apparently ants weren't the only undesirables that infiltrated the inn last night. We need to close the Blackberry for a few days."

"You're sure."

"We don't have a choice. Before she left, 'Mrs. Bolton' erased all of her information from the computer. She's not who she pretended to be."

Thankfully, this was their slow season. The only

immediate reservations they had on the books were for tomorrow and Saturday evening, and they weren't expecting more guests until several of Charity's former residents came in during Christmas week.

Understanding what needed to be done, Molly nodded gravely and moved behind the desk. "I'll cancel the Addams, Crafts and Lamberts with our regrets and suggest a few other places they could stay. I'll also offer them a discount for the next time they stay with us."

Good idea. "Thank you, Aunt Molly."

Beau didn't say a word until Molly had picked up the phone and began speaking. Then he ambled closer to Jenna and lowered his voice. "Would you like to tell me about it now? No pressure. Your choice."

She nodded, knowing what he meant and needing his support. "But first I'd better see what else Mrs. Bolton might've left behind."

Minutes later, Beau watched Jenna rip the huge four-poster bed apart, fierce determination lining her classic features. He fielded the three accent pillows she tossed him and stacked them on a wing chair, then helped her remove the quilted floral spread.

"Want to take the comforter and pillow shams to the hall? They'll need to be dry cleaned before I put them back on the bed."

"Sure," he said. "Whatever you need."

"Thank you. Just toss them on the floor for now." Barely looking up, she pulled off the top sheet and blanket—started tugging up the mattress pad.

He'd just dropped the bedclothes beside the laundry chute when he heard her cry out. He was beside her in an instant. She was staring at the bare mattress. Beau's stomach did a weird little flop. It had been slashed repeatedly, and the incisions had been stuffed with razor blades.

Jenna's blue eyes filled with tears. "He's found me. He's here to finish the job he started two years ago."

Instinct took over, and Beau held her close while his mind spun. She was quaking like an aspen in a windstorm. Any other time, he would've enjoyed having a beautiful woman cling to him, but the fear he'd seen in her eyes was scary. This wasn't the Jenna he'd come to know. She was strong, confident and she didn't fall apart. "You need to call the police," he murmured against her hair.

Nodding, she slowly released her grip on him, then took a defeated walk to the phone on the nightstand. When she'd spoken to Sarah French at the Charity P.D., she hung up, drew a breath and went to the window. Beau followed. He watched her pull back the sheer curtains, nervously scan the sill and frames, then stare down at the backyard.

The temperature had risen, but a few inches of snow remained in the woods behind the inn, some piled on top of her bird feeders where cardinals were hogging the seed. Now a gutsy chickadee gathered his courage and sailed in for his share.

"I've always been a terrible judge of men," she began quietly. "From high school to the workplace, I chose men who weren't right for me. Then I met Courtland Dane at a charity event."

"Fancy name."

Jenna sent him a beaten smile. "Fancy man. He was the CFO of Prime Trust and Investments of Michigan. Are you familiar with it?

Beau shook his head.

"Well, it's big. Not Fortune Five Hundred big, but

big." She swallowed. "Anyway, Court was wealthy, good-looking and charming, and we enjoyed the same things. The theatre…art…music."

"So you accepted when he asked you out."

"Yes. He took me to the opera—*La Bohème*—then to dinner at a spot the rich-and-connected frequent in Detroit. It was a wonderful night, and the next time he called, I said yes again."

She shuddered, and somehow Beau resisted the soul-deep urge to hold her again.

"I should've known there was something off about him. He never talked about family and he didn't seem to have friends, only business associates who were polite, but distant. Then on our fourth date as he was driving me home, he got strange. He seemed to want to change me—mold me into something I wasn't. He suggested that I wear my hair differently and dress in a more so-phisticated way—go heavier on my eye makeup."

Beau scowled. Wealthy or not, the jerk was a loser. What man with a working brain would say that to any woman? Especially one who was as beautifully put to-gether as Jenna was.

"That was my wake-up call. When we got to my apartment, I told him that I wasn't the woman he was looking for, and it was best that we didn't see each other again."

"How did he take it?"

"He got very cool and quiet, but I expected that." She glanced at him, then folded her arms over her chest and stared out again. "I had a problem with my car a few days later. So a friend—one of the student teach-ers from school—followed me to my mechanic's shop so I could drop it off, then drove me back to my apart-ment building. I invited him in for coffee and dessert to thank him. Afterward, I walked him to the door and gave him a hug. Just a friendly, very platonic, thank-you hug."

Her expression grew distant and Beau realized that she was seeing it all unfold again.

"I could hear Mrs. Thompson's TV blaring from behind her closed door. She was watching a game show—*Jeopardy!* Anyway, I watched Malcolm walk to the end of the hall and turn right toward the elevator, then I stepped back inside." She swallowed. "I was closing the door when Courtland forced his way in, shoved me on the floor and kicked the door shut."

Beau's stomach churned. He wasn't sure he wanted to hear any more.

"I'd never seen rage like that," Jenna went on. "His face was—I can't even describe it—and his eyes were blue ice. I tried to get him talking—asked him how he got in. I lived in a secure building."

But "secure" was a relative term. The freak had probably waited near the entrance until another resident stepped out, then slipped inside before the door could lock again.

"He never answered. He started raving, calling me every crude name he could think of and accusing me of sleeping with Mal. He said that he and I had a relationship, and that I'd betrayed him. I was on my feet by then and screaming back that I'd call security if he didn't leave."

She exhaled a shaky breath. "I tried to explain about my car trouble and why Mal was with me, but by that time, he was beyond hearing anything I said. When I ran for the kitchen phone, he pulled a filet knife from the wooden block on the counter."

Beau's stomach fell to his feet.

"He…he did some damage. I don't know how I managed to get across the apartment floor and make it into the hall after losing so much blood. That part's a blur. God was with me, I guess."

God and half of Heaven. Beau spoke softly. "Who found you?"

"Mrs. Thompson. At some point, she came out of her apartment to take her terrier for a walk. Long story short, there were some surgeries and I lost—" She looked away for a long moment, fresh tears welling in her eyes. "I lost my…spleen. But I guess the rest of me is still functional."

The sadness in her voice got to him, and Beau wondered about that pause. Suddenly he was afraid the attack had cost her even more.

"I'm just thankful that Malcolm didn't pay the same price."

"He went after your friend?"

Jenna sent him a wan smile. "No, I'd told him that Mal was a colleague, so he knew we taught at the same school. The next day he…allegedly…smashed the windows out of Mal's cobalt-blue 1966 Chevelle Super Sport. Apparently he'd seen it parked in my space."

"He hurt you, then stuck around long enough to do that?"

"I imagine he thought I was dead until he heard otherwise—and I was in no shape to speak to the police for days. He had time. And now, no one knows where he is. He hasn't been seen since that night two years ago. But men with his kind of money are very capable of hiding. Sometimes in plain sight."

Against his better judgment, Beau took her hand. "You thought you saw him yesterday. The man with the cane."

She nodded. "His features were similar."

"But not exact."

"No. I doubt I would have noticed him until Elmer pointed him out if I hadn't caught him staring at me."

He smiled. "He was probably just admiring a beautiful woman."

She smiled back and murmured her thanks, but he could see that she still had doubts. He squeezed her hand, then released it. "Now, at the risk of sounding like I know what I'm talking about, we should get out of this room in case your guest left fingerprints or other evidence behind for the police. We don't want to mess up an investigation."

Nodding, Jenna combed her fingers through her hair. It slid back to frame her high cheekbones and watery blue eyes. "You're right. Let's wait downstairs. Sarah said Chief Perris would be here shortly."

They didn't have long to wait. She'd barely filled a stunned Aunt Molly in on her disturbing findings when a black-and-white police cruiser pulled into the driveway. A half minute later, Jenna ushered Lon Perris inside. With a nod and clipped "Good morning," he stamped a trace of wet snow from his shoes, and unzipped his fur-collared black uniform jacket. He carried a small aluminum case, and there was a camera slung around his neck.

Everything about Perris was by-the-book, as they said on television police dramas. Everything from the C.P.D. patch on his sleeve, to his severe salt-and-pepper buzz cut, to his military bearing. Years ago he'd lost his battle with teenage acne, and his pockmarked cheeks and black eyes added a menacing look to his features. Former Philadelphia police officer Lon Perris was new to Charity. He'd only held the chief position for six or seven months.

"Thanks for coming," Jenna said, then motioned him toward the curved staircase. "It's the second door on the left at the top of the stairs. As I told Sarah, I probably shouldn't have stripped the bed, but if I hadn't, I wouldn't have found the razor blades."

He didn't respond, just nodded cordially to Beau, ignored Aunt Molly and started up the stairs. Rolling her eyes at the slight, Molly lifted her skirt a few inches and followed.

Jenna looked back at Beau. "Are you coming?" He met her eyes, and despite her nervousness, she felt those undeniable strains of attraction again. Maybe because he'd held and spoken to her with such tenderness. Maybe because he'd called her beautiful.

Straightening from the desk, he shook his head. "No, you can handle Perris. I'm going to take advantage of the inn being empty and make some noisy headway. I'll be in the sitting room when you're through upstairs if you want to talk."

Hiding her disappointment, she nodded and ascended the stairs.

Perris was fast, but hopefully thorough, Jenna decided. Or maybe it didn't take longer than half an hour to process a crime scene. After she'd washed the faint residue of ink from her fingers, she walked into the sitting room. Beau had already removed the pine window molding and sill, and was now prying the baseboards loose.

He set the wedge and cheap pine aside, then rose, dusted his hands on a rag, and ambled over to her. "That was quick. How did it go?"

"All right, I guess. I'm not the best judge."

His brow lined. "I assume he asked if you had enemies."

She nodded. "Right after he asked if anything was missing. I still have to look over the rooms. But yes, he asked if I'd had problems with anyone."

"You told him about the attack?"

"Yes. I gave him the name of the lead investigator in the case and offered to print out an internet photo of Courtland, but he said he'd get what he needed from the Michigan police since he'd be talking to Detective Caspian anyway. He's putting a BOLO out on Courtland—and Mrs. Bolton."

"What about fingerprints?"

She wiggled her fingers. "They were all mine. The room was spotless when Mrs. Bolton arrived, and I was the only one who'd entered it after she checked in."

Jenna sank to a plastic-covered settee, weariness joining the fear she struggled to hide. She studied her clasped hands. "They'll never find her."

Beau matched her quiet tone. "You're a smart woman. You pay attention to detail. I'm sure you gave him enough information to track her down and find out who put her up to this. Provided that she didn't do it on her own."

Startled, Jenna looked up. "On her own?"

He dragged a sawbuck close to her—eased down on the cross beam and linked his hands between the spread of his legs. "I know you're sure that Dane is behind this. But this woman could've had her own reasons—reasons that have nothing to do with you or what happened in Michigan."

"Like what?"

"I don't know. Mental illness? Jealousy? A grudge

against B and Bs in general? When Perris finds her, you'll have your answer."

"I don't see that happening. The only reasonably accurate information I could give him was her height because I'm five-six, and we stood eye to eye. Her weight and hair were guesses. I never saw her out of her bulky jacket and brown wig."

"She wore a wig?"

"And tinted glasses." Suddenly filled with frustration, she got up, needing to walk. "You know, there was a moment while I was checking her in when I had an uneasy feeling about her—partly because of the wig, and the fact that she'd be doing an audit on a Saturday. But I ignored it. I chalked it up to paranoia after having my credit card number stolen. She showed me her driver's license, and the photo looked like her, so that was good enough for—" She stopped abruptly. "Would a DMV photographer allow her to wear a wig for her driver's license photo?"

"Maybe, maybe not. Height and eye color are the only descriptors on PA licenses these days, probably because hair color can change daily. And unless it was a curly red clown's wig, the photographer might not have noticed."

True enough. She might not have noticed it, either, except for the cowlick that drew attention to the wig. Suddenly something else occurred to her. "I just remembered something. She said she was from North Carolina, but she didn't have an accent."

"Then you might want to talk to Perris again. He'll need that information."

Aunt Molly entered the room at a brisk clip. "What that fascist robot needs is a personality!" She turned to Jenna and softened her tone as Beau pushed to his feet. "Forgive me for not coming back after taking that phone call, but I was afraid I'd say something unlady-like to that arrogant boob. What did I miss?"

Jenna squeezed her hand. "No apology necessary, and you didn't miss much. He took my fingerprints for comparison before he dusted the room. All of the prints were mine. Then he took a few more photographs and collected the razor blades. He's hoping to find partial prints, but he's not holding out much hope."

"So he's finished upstairs?"

"For the moment."

"What about the mess he made?"

"We're free to clean it up whenever we want." Jenna moistened her lips. "Who was on the phone?"

"Millie. She said she called yesterday when I was out."

Jenna winced. Yes, she had and she'd forgotten to mention it. "I'm sorry. She wanted to firm up plans for your trip to Hartford. She's really looking forward to your birthday dinner at Chang Chung's."

"Well, that's not going to happen now. I told her that there was too much going on here, and I couldn't get away."

"No," Jenna insisted firmly, "you have to go." Not only had Molly and Millie Wentworth been best friends since elementary school, they were born on the same date. "You two have been planning this for a month."

"We'll celebrate together," Molly assured her. "We'll just do it at a later date."

"Aunt Molly—"

"Jenny, we can talk about this later. Right now, I have a question." Worry deepened the lines in her pixie face. "Did you tell Chief Perris about the couple outside the courthouse?"

"No, because he would've felt obligated to question them, and they're not involved in this. Besides, they have enough on their plates. Promise me you won't mention it to him, either."

"I won't. But I think you should." The phone rang again, and Molly sighed. "I'll get it. So much for this being our slow season. I only wish we were able to accommodate our guests."

Jenna met Beau's eyes across the room. He'd obviously heard their conversation, but he didn't ask who they were talking about because that's the kind of man he was. She was glad of that because she wouldn't have felt comfortable telling him about her exchange with Devona Chandler. A mother's grief over her son's imprisonment didn't need to be discussed. "I should call the station and talk to Perris," she said finally. "Thank you for listening."

"No problem," he said quietly. "Always glad to lend an ear. Or a shoulder."

There it went again—that little blip of awareness. "Likewise," she replied because it was the only thing she could think of. Yet she'd meant it, and that troubled her. The bad boy who'd thrilled then discarded teenage girls when they were in high school was a tall, broad shouldered, good-looking man now. And according to the gossips, his cavalier lifestyle hadn't changed.

Even if she felt confident about dating again—even if she thought it was safe to involve another man in her life—she didn't want to be one of Beau's casualties.

But oh, how she longed to risk it.

Impatient, sick of waiting for the call he'd been expecting, he snagged the disposable cell phone from

the hotel nightstand and pushed the only number programmed into it.

The thin, wiry man answered on the first ring.
"Yes?"

"Have you heard from the woman?"

"She just called. I was about to phone you. She finished her assignment and her credentials have been destroyed."

"Is everything in place?"

"It is."

"Good. I'll expect a delivery to my hotel room tomorrow night. Use a messenger service. I don't want
any of this traced back to me."

SIX

In the rear of his shop in his partitioned-off "clean room," Beau finished buffing the Haskells' sealed oak kitchen cabinets, draped them in plastic, then returned to the business side of his workshop to turn down the thermostat. He congratulated himself on remembering. Because ever since he'd left Jenna this evening, she'd been on his mind.

Identity theft and ants could be explained away, but razor blades were another matter. Of course, there was still a possibility that the Bolton woman was a nutcase who'd been acting alone, and this Dane freak had nothing to do with the vandalism. But if the creep was innocent, then someone really had an axe to grind with Jenna. Were the axe-grinders "the couple outside the courthouse" that Aunt Molly had mentioned? Maybe. Now he wished he'd asked who they were talking about, but he didn't like answering questions about himself, and he did his best to afford others the same courtesy.

Turning off the lights, Beau stepped into the crisp night air and locked his workshop. Strategically directed spotlights showed the way to his house, and with every step he remembered how good it had felt to hold

Jenna close this morning, remembered the light citrus scent of her shampoo.

He'd dated a lot, but like Jenna, he'd failed badly at finding someone to share his life. For a time he'd thought it was Shelley. Strike one. Then Beth had come along, and the abandoned kid in him had gotten so wrapped up in the idea of having a real home and family, he'd missed the signs that said it wasn't going to happen. Strike two.

So despite an attraction to her that nearly took his breath away some days, Jenna couldn't be number three. He wasn't sure he could bounce back from that.

A voice in his head told him to stop wavering—that they were worlds apart.

Beau frowned. Her father had certainly thought so. Years ago, he'd overheard a conversation between Webb Harper and Aunt Molly. He'd gone to the Blackberry's back door to tell his pint-sized savior that they needed gas for the mowers, when he'd heard Harper's quiet voice through the window screen.

"Look, I know he's a nice kid. I like him. I'm sorry he's being raised by a granddad who couldn't care less about him. But he's running with a bunch of thugs, and that kind of thing rubs off. I don't want him hanging around my daughter."

Those words had trampled any notion he'd had of being more to Jenna than the kid who mowed her great-aunt's lawns. So why was he still mulling over that possibility in his mind?

Inside now, he grabbed a glass of milk and a handful of Oreos, then settled into his sparse-but-functional living room. He had the necessities: a TV, a blue plaid sofa, the recliner he was parked in, one lamp and an unfinished end table he'd started for Beth before things had gone belly-up.

He put the TV's remote control to work—then stopped abruptly when the screen filled with a muscle-bound actor who was saying something relevant. Muscleman had decided it was up to him to protect his woman because the local chief of police couldn't find his posterior with both hands.

Beau's uneasiness grew. Perris was lucky to make two-out-of-ten on the personality scale. But was he inept? Could he protect her? And did she even need protection? No one had come after her physically. At the core of things, the only crime that had been committed was vandalism, and Jenna had opened her door to the vandal.

His phone rang. Wondering who was calling this late on a Saturday night, he strode to the wall phone in the kitchen and said hello. He was instantly concerned when he heard Molly Jennings's voice.

"Aunt Molly? Is everything okay?"

"Yes, we're fine. I'm sorry to disturb you at home, but I thought you should know that we've decided to close the Blackberry until Christmas week. That will give us time to look over the entire inn and make certain there are no more surprises. We can't have our guests at risk."

Good idea, but why was she telling him this tonight when they'd probably be seeing each other tomorrow at church? He also wondered why Jenna wasn't doing the calling. "That's probably for the best. It can't hurt to be cautious."

"Exactly. So there won't be any reason for you to keep the noise down when you resume work. You can make as much racket as you like."

"Okay," he said, still curious about the call. "I'll bring a wrecking ball on Monday." But there was always a point to her conversations, and as he expected, she got to it.

"I believe you heard me ask Jenna today about a couple who might want to ruin her business."

"Yes, I did. I also heard you promise not to mention it to anyone."

"No," she returned, "you heard me say I wouldn't mention it to Chief Perris. But Jenny is my world, and I need to share this with someone. Tonight you're it because you care about her, too."

Yeah, he did, even though he had no intention of taking it further.

"Several months ago, Jenny served on a jury and was appointed their foreman. They found the defendant, a twenty-three-year-old with major entitlement issues, guilty of vehicular manslaughter."

He knew this story. It had been in all the papers. The family lived a fair distance away, but the kid's lawyer had requested and received a change of venue because of pre-trial publicity. "You're talking about Lawrence Chandler's son, Tim. He was driving drunk."

"Yes. Are you acquainted with the Chandlers?"

"We're not close, but I know them. I did some work for them a while ago. What happened with Jenna?"

"After the trial, she was walking to her car when Mrs. Chandler came after her. She blamed Jenna for her son being convicted, and even though she lost sleep over it, Jenna didn't see that as a threat."

"But it was?"

"I'm not sure. But when someone tells you in anger that your actions have consequences, it bears considering. Last week, the boy's appeal was denied. I have to believe that with Lawrence Chandler's gas and oil money, and Timothy being their only child, they might've wanted to retaliate in some way."

"You think they hired Mrs. Bolton to trash the Blackberry."

"The timing is certainly right. Better than her belief that that Michigan monster is behind her troubles. When he got angry two years ago, he came after her directly. He didn't send someone else. Why would he change tactics now?"

Maybe because he had to, Beau thought. The guy was still wanted by the police, so if he was smart, he'd keep a low profile.

"Well," she continued when he didn't speak immediately. "That's all I wanted to say. Will we see you at services tomorrow?"

"Yes, I'll be there. Sleep tight, Aunt Molly."

Her voice turned weary. "That's a tall order, young man."

When she'd said good-night and hung up, Beau sighed, considered what she'd told him, then went into his cubbyhole of a home office and dropped into his swivel chair to access the internet. He was being manipulated by a pro, and he knew it. He just wasn't sure what she wanted him to do. Interrogate the Chandlers? Camp out on Jenna's doorstep and turn away anyone who looked suspicious?

He typed in Prime Trust and Investments of Michigan. The site came up. There was no trace or mention of Jenna's nemesis, but one thing was certain about cyberspace. Any information posted there lived on forever.

He typed in Dane's name. A moment later, he was staring at a sharply dressed man in a dark business suit. Jenna's description had been right on the money.

Courtland Dane's eyes were blue ice, though the photographer had tried to show him in a trusting light. Instead he had the look of a cutthroat power broker. High cheekbones in a lean face…salon-cut medium brown hair…narrow, close-to-the-jaw, perfectly trimmed beard and mustache…a smile that barely touched his lips.

Beau sank back in his chair and rocked for a while. Even though a designer suit and pocket silk wouldn't be one of Dane's wardrobe choices now, he looked nothing like the guy they'd seen yesterday at the diner. That made him feel a whole lot better. If Jenna was on some jerk's to-do list, he'd rather it be the Chandlers'. They were well-to-do, well-respected business people—stereotypical pillars of the their community.

He didn't equate them with knives and blood.

Dressed in his collar and Sunday blacks, Reverend Paul Landers was a genial, elderly man with white hair, a bit of a pot belly and kind blue eyes behind rimless bifocals. Landers might not have been the best speaker St. John's congregation had ever heard, but silver-tongued orators had nothing on him when it came to preaching about God's love in today's world.

Jenna listened intently as she sat beside Aunt Molly, feeling as though he were speaking to her personally. She was aware of Beau's presence in the pew behind her as the reverend wrapped up his sermon.

"So on those days when life gets to be too much, remember this: our Father in Heaven wants us to be joyful. And there's a difference between happiness and joy. Happiness is the result of a happening. Joy is the little candle in our hearts that celebrates life."

He folded his hands on the oak dais and smiled. "Your job makes you crazy? We've all been there. I was an accountant before I was a pastor." He glanced around. "You've had a disagreement with a friend, co-worker or family member, or you're dealing with a problem that seems to have no solution? Well, if you've done everything in your power to resolve it, but nothing you do is working…you have to give it to God and move on. Don't let people and events over which you have no control steal your joy. Joy is God's gift to us. We shouldn't squander it."

No, we shouldn't, Jenna thought. But sometimes it was unavoidable.

Raising his hands, the reverend brought everyone to their feet. "Now let's all lift our voices—in joy."

Minutes later, Beau eased into step beside her as organist Emma Lucille Bridger segued smoothly from "How Great Thou Art" into a pleasant recessional hymn, and the congregation filed out, smiling, chatting and shaking hands. He smiled at her, and the message in his eyes was clear. It was the same message Aunt Molly offered as the three of them walked toward the parking lot.

As she did every Sunday during the cold weather, her tiny aunt wore street clothes beneath her black faux-Persian-lamb coat and pillbox hat. "The reverend made a lot of sense today," she said in an undertone as she pulled on her gloves. "I hope you were listening closely."

"I was," Jenna replied.

"But did you take his sermon to heart?"

Jenna glanced around, hoping that no one was close enough to overhear. She didn't want to answer questions—not even from sympathetic friends. She was saved from replying when her aunt caught sight of Delores Buck and her friend Donna, and said she'd see Jenna in the car.

"Saved by the bell?" Beau asked.

Jenna smiled a little. "For the moment, anyway." If she'd been pressed to answer, she would've said that she'd taken the sermon to heart as much as she could. Because even on this sunny Sunday morning surrounded by friends and acquaintances, she was glad to have a tall, well-built guardian nearby. She was about to invite him back to the inn for a potluck brunch when the well-dressed Killians, Frank and his sister Barbara, strode past them with a cool look and a curt "Good morning."

She and Beau returned their greeting, then with her spirits dipping, Jenna watched the Killians head toward a new Dodge truck with crossed hammers on the door. A light breeze lifted Frank's shoulder-length hair. *Give it to God, and move on,* she told herself silently. *You did what had to be done.*

Beau spoke in an undertone as they approached their vehicles. "He started the work in the sitting room, didn't he?"

Jenna replied quietly, an apology in her tone. "Yes, but you need to know that you were our first choice. There were extenuating circumstances that I'd rather not go into."

He waved off her concerns. "Not a problem."

"Thanks. Would you like to join us for brunch?" She smiled. "Or are the Cowboys playing at one o'clock?"

"Actually, they play tonight. But I promised to help a friend square up some walls. Thanks, though." He opened the Liberty's door for her. "Another time?"

She liked the sound of that. "Yes, another time."

"Great. I'll see you tomorrow."

Three hours later, ten minutes after Aunt Molly left to visit a friend who'd moved to Holy Savior Elder Care, the doorbell chimed. Jenna felt a rush of uneasiness, then sighed. Killers didn't ring doorbells. Abandoning her second thorough search of the Blue Room, she went downstairs, checked the security monitor and quickly unlocked the front door.

"Hi," she said, hoping she didn't look as pleased as she felt. "Come in."

Grinning, Beau stepped inside. "Thanks. I'm a little early to start work, but if you're busy, I could come back in seventeen or eighteen hours."

Some of that joy Reverend Landers had talked about bubbled up in her, and Jenna laughed. "Don't go. I wasn't busy. I was being obsessive." He raised his eyebrows, but she ignored the question there. "Now that you're here, though, it seems like a good time to take a break." She motioned for him to follow her through the wide doorway and into the hall. "Coffee?"

"Yeah, thanks. But only if you're having some."

"I am." They entered the kitchen. "So," she said. "You were just in the neighborhood and decided to drop in?"

"No, I'd just finished helping Randy Caruthers square up the bathroom walls in his new place, and was leaving the Quick Stop when Aunt Molly pulled up to the self-serve pumps." He chuckled. "I'm still trying to figure out why a woman who's barely big enough to fill the glove box drives a half ton Suburban."

"Join the club."

"Anyway, while I was gassing up her car, she mentioned that she was headed for the nursing home so I thought I'd see if you were as bored as I was." He met her eyes and got serious. "Or worried."

Jenna's uneasiness came back, coupled with disappointment. So this was a keep-an-eye-on-Jenna visit, probably prompted by her aunt? How flattering. "Thank you, but I'm fine."

She filled two mugs from the carafe on the counter, handed Beau his black coffee then added cream and sugar to hers. He'd commandeered a tall stool from under the butcher-block work island; Jenna chose the stool across from him and reached for conversation. The topic she chose was just asking for more disappointment, but she couldn't help herself. Yesterday he'd held her, and she'd felt safe and warm. But when evening came she'd found herself wondering if he was already holding someone else.

"So how was your Saturday night?"

"Not too bad," he returned. "I got twelve cabinets ready for delivery to a customer over in McKean County, then put together a pretty fair gourmet dinner."

"Really? You cook?"

His dark eyes twinkled. "Don't look so shocked. I can do more than wreck a room."

"My apologies," she said, laughing and liking this side of him. "What did you make?"

He sent her a cheeky grin. "Milk and Oreos."

Jenna felt her smile stretch. "And was that for one or two, Chef Travis?"

"Only one, but I had two helpings. What about you? What did you do last night while everyone else in town was out to dinner, bowling or seeing a movie?"

She made a face. "I scattered a half dozen more ant traps around in the kitchen and Blue Room—although the ants seem to be gone now. I guess it wasn't a typical date night for either of us."

"Guess not. Do you miss it?"

"Do I miss…dating?"

"Yeah."

Lowering her eyes, she ran a fingertip around the rim of her mug and answered truthfully. "Yes, but that ship has sailed—at least until my life gets less complicated. The attack left scars—emotional and physical. Every day I see them is a reminder that I have to be careful." She forced a happy lilt into her voice. "You, on the other hand, can date to your heart's content."

"And according to the grapevine, I do?"

"I didn't say that."

Beau blew out a dry laugh and took a sip of his coffee. "Don't believe everything you hear. It's been…" He thought for a moment. "Four months since I've seen anyone."

Four months? "Can I ask why?"

"Sure. Because I wasn't enjoying myself. After two serious relationships that didn't work out, I felt like I was just going through the motions—conducting interviews."

The man was full of surprises. "Isn't that what dating is?"

"I suppose. But it has to be fun, too, and that wasn't happening, so I'm on a break." He flashed a smile. "Speaking of fun, when this is all over, you should take a vacation. Go on a cruise. Buy a cowboy hat and check into a dude ranch."

She smiled back. "People who run B and Bs don't take vacations. We are the vacation."

"You could still get away for a short one—at least for a day. In fact, when the weather breaks, we should take an afternoon and go geocaching. Have you ever done that?"

Jenna's pulse quickened. Was he asking her for a

date? Or was this another un-date to watch over her or get her out of the inn? "No, but I understand it's like a treasure hunt. People hide boxes full of trinkets in scenic areas, then post the coordinates on an internet site, right? The outdoor club at the Michigan school where I taught went a few times. The kids liked it."

"You will, too. Well, if you decide to go. There's a pretty nice cache called The Hideaway out near Payton's Rocks. It's fairly easy to get to—less than a mile walk from the road."

"And that's why it's 'pretty nice'?" she teased.

"No," he replied with a patient smile, "it's nice because it's a historic site. In the late 1800s it was a railway depot. The tracks are gone—it's a snowmobile trail now, and there's not much left of the stone walls. But it's still worth seeing. We can park nearby, then I'll plug the coordinates into my GPS, and you can take it from there."

Unbidden, Jenna's anxiety returned. For a few moments, the idea of trekking through the woods with him had been exciting. When she was in high school, she, Rachel and Margo had loved hiking the trails at Payton's Rocks. But now that Beau seemed to think this outing was a sure thing, the thought of walking, unprotected, through tall stands of trees, huge rocks and thick laurels had her heart racing. There were too many places of concealment.

When she didn't reply, his smiled faltered and understanding seemed to dawn. Beau lowered his voice. "Jenna, you can't stay holed up in here forever, missing out on everything life has to offer. If you do, Dane—or whoever's doing this to you—wins. Is that what you want?"

Of course not. She missed the freedom she'd had

before the attack. But she'd been living in a well of fear and uncertainty for so long, the idea of stepping outside her comfort zone was almost terrifying.

"Isolating yourself isn't doing you any good. So say yes. Spring's a long way off, so you'll have plenty of time to get used to the idea." Reaching across the butcher-block tabletop, he smiled and tugged a lock of her hair. "And there's one more selling point I think bears repeating."

She warmed at his touch. "What's that?"

"I'll be with you."

He was right, she realized finally. She was still anxious. But she had to stop being so afraid of dying that she was afraid to live. What a terrible waste of a life that would be.

"Thank you," she murmured.

"For what?"

"For the push. I'd love to go geocaching with you in the spring."

He smiled. "Good. Now if I can push a little harder... take a drive with me on Wednesday. I plan to work here until noon or so, then pick up the cabinets I mentioned and make a delivery. I wouldn't mind having some company. I'll even spring for supper."

She surprised both of them by accepting immediately. "What time would you like to leave?"

It was nearly eight o'clock when Beau climbed out of the shower, toweled off, then slipped into sweatpants and a T-shirt and padded into his kitchen. He opened the refrigerator and frowned. If he didn't shop for groceries soon, he'd starve to death. He wasn't in the mood for eggs or hot dogs, and the leftover slices of ham he'd bought at the deli last week were headed south. Finally, he grabbed a can of soda, shut the fridge and opened his cupboards. Five minutes later, he was pouring boiling water over a foam cup of ramen noodles, jamming a spoon inside and sealing it up again to cook. He picked up his college-dorm supper and headed for the living room.

He should've accepted Aunt Molly's invitation to stay for an early dinner. But she'd looked tired when she came back from her visit, and he'd needed time to work on the new nativity stable he was making for the church's Christmas display.

Liar.

Scowling, he put his soup and soda on the end table and dropped into his recliner. Okay. Neither of those were the reason he'd left when Molly came home. He'd suddenly regretted asking Jenna to make that delivery with him. He'd only wanted her to leave the inn once in a while—live life, not hide from it. Now he was getting caught up in something that could only end with another big, fat hole in his gut. Worse, he didn't have the sense to step back.

He turned on the TV—clicked through a zillion channels without finding anything interesting, then settled for the all-Elvis channel on Sirius radio until the Cowboys game came on at eight o'clock. A funny kind of loneliness slipped in, and he wondered if he should get a dog.

That's when it hit him.

He was as much a prisoner of his brand of solitude as Jenna was.

SEVEN

At nine-fifteen on Tuesday morning, Jenna answered Aunt Molly's call to come down to the foyer. She'd been trying to stay busy for two days, but no matter how much energy she'd put into cleaning and vacuuming, she'd failed to keep the memories at bay. Today was November seventeenth. Two years ago today, she'd been lying in a critical care unit, fighting for her life.

Seeing Rachel Campbell standing at the bottom of the stairs was exactly the pick-me-up she needed. "Rachel," she said, giving her friend a hug. "Nice to see you. Not that you need an excuse, but what brings you to our humble abode?"

When Aunt Molly made a hasty departure, Jenna knew why Rachel was there. Her aunt had been on the telephone. "She told you about the ants."

"And the razor blades. I wish you'd called me. Did you tell Margo?"

"No, and I hope you don't, either."

"Jenna, she'd want to know."

"I realize that, but there's nothing either of you can do about this. Besides, she and Cole need to focus on the case they're working. Now take off your jacket and let's talk about something fun."

With a patiently disgruntled look, Rachel shrugged out of her down-filled white parka and handed it over. "You're wrong. I could have listened. It wasn't that long ago that you were there for me."

Jenna hung the jacket in the closet. "I know. And I would've appreciated having your support. But you have a brand-new husband to spoil and a business to run."

"Not for long. The business part is winding down. The cabins will be empty after deer season, then we're shutting down the campground and snuggling in until spring."

Snuggling in. That sounded absolutely sublime, and once again, the memory of Beau holding her made her miss his strength and his tenderness.

Be careful, a tiny voice cautioned. *You're getting too attached, and there are at least three good reasons to keep your distance.*

Didn't she know it.

With a quick smile, Jenna linked her arm through Rachel's. "Come on. Let's grab something to drink from the kitchen, then find a soft place to sit and talk. I missed seeing you and Jake at services on Sunday."

"We'd planned to go, but something came up. I'll tell you about it a little later. Right now, I'd rather talk about you. What's being done to find this 'Mrs. Bolton'?"

Jenna gave her what little information she had while they filled a tray with tea and assorted cookies, then declared the subject off limits for the duration of Rachel's visit. After placing the tray on the parlor's dark oak coffee table, Jenna joined Rachel on the sofa. Despite its formal appearance, the turquoise-and-gold brocade settee was comfortable.

She loved what Aunt Molly had done with this room.

The turquoise-and-gold colors were repeated in the wallpaper and accented by deep greens and creams. Heavy damask draperies in hunter green were held back with gold braided tassels, letting in the sun's rays, and lighting a wall of shelves filled with books, antique pieces and framed family photographs. Long Persian rugs lay scattered on the dark hardwood floor, every-where but in front of the brick fireplace.

"I'm glad you came over today," Jenna said, picking up the china teapot and pouring. "I've been thinking about those self-defense classes you mentioned last week, and if it's not too late to sign up, let's do it. We haven't taken a class together since high school."

Rachel winced prettily because there was no other way for her to do it. Her friend was a natural beauty with a peaches-and-cream complexion, and a razor-cut sable shag that framed her cheekbones and called to attention the dark-lashed, sea-green of her eyes. Today she wore a soft, fuzzy, white cowl-neck sweater that made her features even more striking.

"About those classes," Rachel said with some reluctance. "I won't be taking them after all. I'll be doing something else."

Jenna smiled to hide her disappointment. "That's okay. Are you and Jake taking a trip?"

Rachel laughed softly. "Oh, it's going to be a trip all right. But we're not going anywhere." Her eyes brimmed with happiness. "Jen, you didn't see me at church yesterday because I was a little under the weather. We're pregnant."

"Oh, Rachel, how wonderful!" She hugged her friend close. "Jake must be thrilled."

"He is. We both are."

"Do you know it it's a boy or girl?"

"No. We want to be surprised when the baby gets here."

Jenna hugged Rachel again, visions of tiny, sweet-smelling babies filling her mind. But then thoughts that had no place in this celebration intruded, reminding her that she might never know the joy Rachel was feeling. Her gynecologist had tried to reassure her that pregnancy was still possible since she continued to have regular periods—insisted that her remaining ovary and attached fallopian tube were healthy. But as she'd heard the heroine of a movie once say, bad news was easier to believe.

"Time for a toast," she said, purging that thought. "You call Aunt Molly downstairs, and I'll fill the champagne flutes."

"Jen, I can't have—"

Jenna touched a fingertip to Rachel's lips. "Hush. I know what I'm doing."

They were all laughing, talking and hugging when Beau walked into the parlor a few minutes later. "You ladies are having way too much fun this early in the morning. What's going on?"

"We're celebrating life," Aunt Molly answered, grinning from ear-to-ear as she moved past him. "Stay where you are. I'll be right back."

He looked blankly at Jenna. "You're celebrating life?"

Smiling, she indicated the three milk-filled flutes on the coffee table. "Not just life. New life."

He couldn't have looked more pleased. Beau took Rachel's hand. "Congratulations. How's Jake feel about it?"

"He's delirious."

"I would be, too." He began to chuckle then. "The

two of you have come a long way since he asked me to hang that steel door on your camp store. He thought you'd serve him his head on a plate when you got back from Williamsburg."

Rachel laughed softly. "I nearly did. But that was May, this is November, and as you can see, I got over it."

Aunt Molly reappeared and put a flute in Beau's hand. "Okay, Jenny. We're ready. Do the honors."

Jenna smiled as they lifted their glasses, then proceeded with all the heartfelt sincerity she could express. "To Rachel, Jake and their sweet baby-to-be. No child will ever be loved more."

An hour and a half later, Beau went to the door across the hall from the sitting room and knocked lightly. Aunt Molly had taken the morning paper upstairs to her quarters, and the inn was strangely quiet. He waited for another moment, then decided that Jenna had opted for a little R&R, too. He was about to walk when he heard a sound that made his chest tighten. She was crying.

He fought with himself for a long moment, weighing the wisdom of knocking again. Then he did it. This time she came to the door. She looked composed, but her red nose and the glassy shine in her eyes told him he hadn't been mistaken.

"Hey," he said softly. "Are you okay?"

"Of course. Why wouldn't I be?"

"I'm not sure. But you seemed fine when I got here, and now you're not." No one had phoned, the mail hadn't arrived with bad news and the only person who'd visited was Rachel. And her news was as good as it got.

Or was it?

Beau took a moment to decide whether to jump into her life with both boots, or back off. His radar told him she'd prefer that he did the latter. "Okay," he said. "It's none of my business. But if you feel like talking, I'll be around." He drew a breath. "In the meantime, I'm taking a break and heading for the diner. Can I bring something back for you or Aunt Molly?"

"Nothing for me, thanks, and Aunt Molly said she'll eat when she's hungry. I guess we're both still full of cookies."

"Okay, I won't be long." He started away, then hesitated. "I think Rachel enjoyed the fuss you made over her this morning. That was a nice touch, toasting her baby news with milk."

She nodded and smiled, but he could see that her tears were close again. So he did the only thing that felt right for both of them. He said, "See you in a little while," and walked away.

When he returned at one o'clock, she was her calm, together self again. Earlier, she'd been in a purple fleece tracksuit. Now she wore brown knitted leggings and a cream-colored tunic with a long, loosely tied jute belt studded with tiny brown stones and gold circles. Gold hoop earrings showed under her sun-streaked blond hair.

She stepped into the sitting room and set a mug of hot coffee on his worktable. "For you."

"Thank you. But why?"

"Because I made you uncomfortable today, and I'm sorry."

"No problem. I just wish I could've helped. I never know what to do when a woman cries."

She smiled a little. "My dad used to say that any man

fifth birthday celebration with her best friend from school." He shrugged. "She can do it next year, I suppose. Provided they're both still around."

Jenna's gaze sharpened. "You're bullying me into accepting?"

"No. I'm just trying to give you *and* Aunt Molly what you both want."

Twenty minutes later, Beau had gone back to work, and Jenna was on the phone with Kari Young at the community center. The self-defense class started this Thursday and consisted of four three-hour sessions, but if Jenna preferred to wait, they'd be having another class after the holidays. She didn't want to wait. By the time she'd pushed the disconnect button and gone upstairs again, she no longer felt as though she'd been forced to make that call. She felt good about it.

She tapped at the partially open door to her great-aunt's quarters, then poked her head inside. Aunt Molly looked up from the creamy brocade wing chair across from her matching sofa. She was wearing her glasses— a rarity—and the morning newspaper lay open on the coffee table.

Jenna came inside and closed the door, and Aunt Molly peered at her over her lenses. "Registration was still open?"

She lowered herself to the sofa. "Yes. Classes are Thursday and Friday this week, then finish up on Monday and Tuesday of next week. Now will you please call Millie and tell her to meet your plane on Friday night?"

"You're sure about this?" Molly asked, the creases in her face deepening.

"I'm sure." But as soon as her aunt was in the air,

she'd absolve Beau of his duties and let him live his life. She had no intention of being an albatross around his neck.

Gripping the arms of the chair, Molly pushed to her feet, then studied Jenna for a beat. "Very well, but I want your solemn promise that you won't back out of this agreement. I won't go if you're planning to send Beau packing as soon as my plane takes off."

Jenna stilled. Was she that transparent, or was Aunt Molly reading minds these days? Either way, she was stuck. "I promise."

"Good. Now, while I'm talking to Millie, you should read the article under the Community Happenings banner on page three." She headed for her bedroom telephone. "Apparently it's the second time the announcement's run. I can't imagine how I missed it before."

"What announcement?"

"Read, dear."

Spinning the newspaper around to face her, Jenna scanned the headline and first two lines of text—and smiled.

Charity's First Annual Fruitcake Fling. Did you re-gift that fruitcake you got last Christmas? Is the recipient now using it for a doorstop? Then it's time to fling a few for charity.

Jenna glanced through the doorway to her aunt's room. "Fling a few?"

Molly picked up the receiver and dialed. "It seems that folks in Manitou Springs, Colorado, have been tossing fruitcakes for years. Keep reading."

When her aunt returned to the sitting room a few minutes later, Jenna had finished the article. It was a great idea. Instead of waiting until January, the event would be held on the Saturday before Thanksgiving so proceeds from the fundraiser would be available to the food bank in time for both Thanksgiving and Christmas deliveries. The rules were simple. The fruitcakes had to be edible, and loaf-size only, and the entry fee was five dollars plus one canned or non-perishable food item. There were three categories: flinging, catapulting and launching. The first, second and third place contestants whose fruitcakes flew the farthest would receive gift certificates from local merchants. But at day's end, Jenna knew the real winners would be the food bank and local residents who needed a helping hand.

"What do you think?" Molly asked.

"I think it's wonderful. My only problem is the timing. You'll be in Connecticut."

"Then you'll go with Beau," she said, then moved along. "Now, we'll need to bake a few to fling, but the Chamber would also like folks to donate a few extras to sell at the event." She pursed her lips. "I believe a dozen will do. Just give me a minute to change, and we can be off to the market for candied fruit. Unless you'd rather stay here."

Jenna smiled, loving her aunt's energy. "No, I'll go with you." And while Molly shed her silk and velveteen for more conventional attire, she'd grab their coats. Not only would donating to a worthy cause make Jenna feel good, baking would be a distraction from the uneasy images that continued to plague her mind. Between those and thoughts of the tall man cutting oak trim on the Blackberry's enclosed back porch, there was little room in her head for anything else.

At nine o'clock that night, Jenna stood in her semi-dark sitting room and looked out on the white gazebo her father had built when she was a child. Years before they'd all faced fearful events, she, Rachel and Margo had played there like innocents, then later, gathered there to whisper about boys, shed tears and celebrate the milestones they'd reached. Life had been so simple then. Now they were grown women and those gazebo days were gone. A melancholy flood of nostalgia hit her, and suddenly she felt an overwhelming need to reconnect with friends. She hoped it wasn't too late for a phone call.

Slipping off the purple robe that matched her nightgown, Jenna draped it over a chair and got into bed. There was a rustle of puffy satin comforter as she shifted to stack her pillows against the antique headboard, then picked up the handset and dialed.

Margo answered her cell phone on the second ring. "It's about time you called, stranger," she said, and Jenna could picture her warm smile. "How are things in snowy Pennsylvania?"

"Wet and slushy. How are things in sunny Florida?"

"Strange as it sounds, not much warmer than your temperatures in Charity. The farmers are nervous about their orange groves. They've been lighting their smudge pots at night."

"That's not good. How's the case coming?"

"Pretty well. We're hoping to wrap it up soon so we can get home for Thanksgiving at my mom's house. Cole's whole family is coming in."

Jenna felt an emotional tug in her chest. Considering the past few days, she wouldn't be seeing her mother, and her dad had been gone for years. "Sounds like a good time."

"It will be if you like noise. You and Aunt Molly should join us if you don't have other plans."

"Thanks, but we do. We're helping out at St. John's. The church is hosting this year's dinner for area singles and seniors—actually anyone who'll be alone or can't be with their families."

"Oh, that's right. My mom mentioned it. Well, let's get together before the holiday then. Even if Cole stays on for a few days, I want to get home early to help Mom get ready for the mob. She's planning to do a lot of baking. How about Monday afternoon? I'll pick up Rachel and we'll come over to the Blackberry."

"Oh, Margo, I'd love that."

"Great. So what's new in Charity?"

For a long second, Jenna thought about telling her— then didn't. That news could wait until next week. "Fruitcakes," she said, lightly. "We made six today, and we'll probably bake another six tomorrow. The Chamber of Commerce has a fun event planned for this Saturday."

He tipped the messenger, then opened the package, and carried the device to the desk in his room. The note inside was brief and concise. "Nine hours. Various sites." He pulled out a chair and sat, started the recording.

Time stretched, and with every hour he got more agitated, first with the content, then with the sound quality. There were better voice-activated bugs on the market, but they had to be retrieved to collect information, and he'd known that wouldn't be possible. She rarely left the inn, and when she did, her aunt was there. Recording her from a distance was his only option. He just hoped the gray van and beige sedan weren't attracting too much attention.

Walking to the far side of the room, he opened the

drapes, then turned off the lamps and returned to the long window overlooking the city's light show. He let the recording play. Some conversations were too faint to understand, and others set his teeth on edge. Suddenly he heard something that spiked his interest, and quickly returning to the desk, he clicked on the lamp, backed up the recording and listened again. Yes. This was what he'd been hoping for.

He now had a plan.

EIGHT

When Jenna walked into the sitting room with Beau's coffee the next morning, he was on his cell phone. Mouthing "sorry," she put it on his worktable and started away. He followed and beckoned her back. It only took a moment for her to realize he was talking to Officer Larry "Fish" Troutman at the Charity P.D.

"Yeah, Fish, I have some idea, but I can't be sure. I heard what I thought were shots last Friday night, but when I went out to look around, everything around my place seemed fine." He walked to the window and looked out. "Yeah, that's what I thought. Someone outlawing deer, or a car backfiring. I only saw the bullet holes in my sign this morning."

Jenna felt a jolt. Bullet holes?

Fish said something, and Beau replied. "I took the sign down. But I didn't touch the slugs in the wall behind it." He paused again. "Yeah, I'd appreciate that. I'm at the Blackberry doing some work for Jenna. I'll be here all day." Then with a cordial, "Thanks, Fish," he tucked his phone away and sent her a smile. "Good morning."

Jenna sent him a blank stare. "How can it be a good morning when someone's shooting at you?"

"Not me. The sign on my workshop."

"That doesn't upset you?"

"I don't like it, but I did my share of damage to streetlights and stop signs when I was a stupid kid. If someone wanted to send me a message, they would've shot through my windows." He grinned. "Besides, I don't have enemies. I'm lovable."

Jenna melted inside. He certainly was.

"So what's this?" he said, glancing at the mug on his worktable. "Coffee for me again?"

She sent him a weary look. "It's the least I can do considering what you're giving up to babysit me."

"Giving up?" His dark eyes twinkled. "Oh. You must be talking about Charity's pulsing nightlife. The flashing neon lights, the fast-paced club scene."

Jenna sent him a patient look. "You know what I mean. This isn't right. You shouldn't have to give up your evenings because of me. In fact, if you have a chance to go out, there's no reason why I can't stay at Rachel's for a while. I'm sure that would satisfy our promise to Aunt Molly."

Beau sighed. "Are you finished?"

"Yes."

"Then relax. I'm not the man that you and half the town think I am. I told you the truth before. I'm not seeing anyone, and no one's seeing me. The only evening plans I have this week are with you. Okay?"

Jenna couldn't stop a timid smile. "Okay. Drink your coffee before it gets cold."

"Wait. Where are you off to?"

"Not far. Just out to the foyer. I'm expecting my mom to call back. She phoned a little while ago, but had to hang up when a friend came to her door."

"Did you tell her what was going on?"

"No. She'd want to be here, and that would just give me one more person to worry about." When he said he understood, she continued. "Was there something you wanted to discuss?"

"Yeah, there is." He nodded at the narrow stack of wood lined up against the long wall. "The trim's all cut, but I'd like to stain and varnish it at my shop so you don't have to deal with the fumes. Which brings me to the sander. I'll seal the room the best I can, but there's going to be a lot of dust. Are there any respiratory issues I should know about?"

Was he thinking about her attack and the "damage" she'd alluded to? "With me? No, thank heaven."

"Great, then if there's time, I'll start the floor on Friday after we drop Aunt Molly off at the airport."

That stopped her in her tracks. "You're going with us?"

"Driving her yourself sort of defeats the purpose of my hanging out here since you'd be coming home in the dark." He hesitated, seeming to examine other solutions. "She could drive herself, I guess, and leave her SUV in the lot. She's more than capable."

Yes, she was. But that meant there would be no one there to see her off—no one to wish her a great birthday trip and hug her goodbye. That didn't feel right.

Jenna met Beau's eyes. He was smiling. But it wasn't a yeah-I'm-manipulating-you smile. It was just…sweet and caring. A warm glow spread through her, and Jenna smiled back. Maybe his offer to play bodyguard wasn't totally for Aunt Molly's peace of mind. Maybe he wanted to see where this attraction was headed. In spite of her reservations, that made two of them. "Well, then. I guess there will be three of us on the road Friday afternoon."

The day went smoothly. Jenna spoke to her mom and made tentative plans to get together after Thanksgiving, though Gayle Harper was disappointed that she wouldn't see her only child on the big day. She was glad Jenna would be serving meals at St. John's, though, because now that they wouldn't be together she'd be doing the same at the Salvation Army's homeless shelter. It was a warm, feel-good conversation, without any mention of ants or credit card fraud or secret fears, and Jenna didn't feel guilty in the least for keeping those things from her.

Then the hang-ups began.

By the time Fish pulled in to talk with Beau about the bullet holes in his sign, Jenna was totally on edge. Baking fruitcakes had been therapeutic yesterday. It wasn't working today.

She ushered Fish Troutman inside before he could ring the bell. "Hey, Jenna," he said, removing his flat campaign hat.

"Hi, Fish."

Troutman was a tall, lanky young man in his mid-twenties with an agreeable personality, fire-red hair and loads of fading freckles. He flashed her a smile full of silver braces. "You and Mrs. Jennings baking today? Something smells good."

"Fruitcakes. Would you like a slice?"

He grimaced. "No, thanks. Is Beau around? He said he'd be here all day."

"Yes, he's in the sitting room." She motioned him through the doorway to the hall. "It's the door on the right. Just follow the country music on the radio. And Fish? When you're through talking with him, I need to speak to you."

A look of concern crossed his face. "Did something else happen? The chief probably told you that we haven't had a hit on that BOLO yet."

"No, he hasn't gotten back to me since we spoke. But I've had three hang-up calls this morning, and I'm a little anxious about it."

"You got Caller ID?"

"Yes, but the only thing that comes up on the display is 'Out of Area.'"

"Okay," he said soberly. "Let's talk more about this after I see Beau."

"Thank you. I'll be in the kitchen."

When he entered the kitchen a few minutes later, Beau was with him. With Aunt Molly busy upstairs in the turret room, Jenna took the last two loaves of fruitcake from the oven, placed them on a cooling rack, then pulled off her oven mitts. She spoke to Beau. "Everything okay?"

He exchanged a long, tentative glance with Fish before he answered. "Yeah, no problem. It was probably just kids. What about these hang-ups? Fish said you were concerned."

"I don't know," she replied, wondering about that look. "The moment I answer, someone breaks the connection, or the line's already dead. I nearly called the phone company to request a number change until I remembered that we won't be in business long if our guests can't reach us."

"Any chance the calls were from telemarketers?"

"I don't see how. We're on a no-call list."

"Yeah, well, that cuts down on a lot of them," Fish said, "but it doesn't include charities. You know how these calls work, right? Solicitors use computers to dial numbers. If the computer reaches somebody, the call's routed to a sales rep. But if all the sales reps are busy on other lines, the computer hangs up. I can't tell you how many times last week we heard from folks who thought they were being harassed."

Jenna drew a hopeful breath. "They received more than a few hang-ups?"

"One lady had five. Like I said, they're probably from charities. With Thanksgiving and Christmas coming up, a lot of them are asking for help."

Beau took a slow walk toward her. "Feeling better about this now?"

She nodded, but somewhere inside she was still uneasy. She was almost certain she'd heard someone breathing on the line before the third hang-up. Although by that time, she was already on edge, so it might've been her imagination. "Thanks, Fish."

"You're welcome." He went to the side door, then stepped outside. "But if you keep getting these calls, let us know. Maybe we can get some numbers from the phone company—see what's up. "

"I will. And if there's any progress on the other matter—"

"I'll let you know." He was heading for his black-and-white when he turned around and prepared to say something else—then changed his mind and kept walking.

Was he questioning those hang ups, too? Jenna wondered as she watched him leave. Her apprehension rose a notch. If so, that wasn't very comforting.

It was midafternoon when Beau found Aunt Molly in the foyer, buttoning her long wool coat and preparing to meet the ladies of her bridge club. "I just tapped at Jenna's door, but no one answered. Do you know where she is?"

"Yes, I do. She's up in the attic. Apparently, she's at loose ends today and needs something to occupy her mind. She's decided to start decorating for Christmas."

"Rushing the season a little, isn't she?"

"Only by a few days." Molly pulled a floppy purple knitted hat over her short white hair, then picked up her black handbag and dug out her keys. "We're generally decorated by Thanksgiving day. Makes the place look festive for our guests." She sighed. "Well, when we have guests."

She walked briskly to the door, then let herself out. The sun was actually shining for a change. "Go on up. I'm sure she could use some help with those boxes."

"Thanks. I will. Do you want me to reset the alarm?"

"No, dear. I can do that from out here. See you in a little while."

Beau watched her leave, then climbed the attic stairs and called for Jenna. If she was still on edge, he didn't want to add to her uneasiness by sneaking up on her. He'd reached the attic floor.

"I'm over here," she returned, and he followed the sound of her voice.

He'd been up here before, but only long enough to deposit and drape the small pieces of furniture from the sitting room. Now he really took it in. The lack of dust and disorganized mayhem surprised him.

She looked pretty sitting on an old steamer trunk near the window with a dozen boxes in front of her. Light from the afternoon sun lit the golden streaks in her hair. She wore simple black earrings that matched the white-and-black snowflake pattern on the thigh-length sweater she wore with black leggings. As always a gold cross hung from a chain around her neck.

"Aunt Molly said you want to start decorating for Christmas."

"Only the artificial tree we put up in the parlor. I have the time, so I might as well use it."

"Artificial? You're joking."

"Nope. No joke. There hasn't been a real tree in the parlor for years. Between guests with allergies and the mess from the needles, I think Aunt Molly just gave up. We do put a real one up in the sitting room. It's a smaller space, so the pine scent really fills the room. I love it."

A hollow spot opened in Beau's chest with the mention of Christmas trees, but he forced himself to stay focused. He indicated the boxes in the center of the floor. "Do you want these carried downstairs?"

"Not quite yet. I still have some sorting to do. But if you want to hang around for a few minutes, I wouldn't mind some help with the tree. It's huge." She opened a box of pink glass balls and thin crystal angels—smiled as she lifted one to the light. "I always pick out my favorites first. You know, the special ornaments that have meaning."

No, he didn't know, but he nodded anyway. Jasper hadn't been big on Christmas trees—or for that matter, Christmas itself. The truth was, he could fill a book with things Jasper hadn't liked, and his name would've topped the list. "Mind if I walk around and be nosy? You've got some neat stuff up here."

"Not at all. Most of it belongs to Aunt Molly and Uncle Charles." Her voice softened. "My mom and dad had a good marriage, but Aunt Molly and Uncle Charles's was like a fairy tale." Rising, she walked along the outside wall, passing stacks of hatboxes, a dressmaker's dummy and an old peddle sewing machine on the way. She stopped beside a caddy where garment bags hung, then unzipped one of them and beckoned him closer. "Take a peek."

Beau looked, then felt slightly uneasy—almost as though he were intruding on someone's private life. There was a vintage military uniform inside. Coat, pants and a billed hat. Jenna's great-uncle had been a decorated World War II officer.

She opened another garment bag where a time-yellowed satin wedding gown and veil hung in front of a man's dark suit. Tucked inside the jacket, an old white shirt wore a broad striped necktie, onyx tie tack and matching cufflinks.

Jenna zipped the bags back up and smiled fondly. "She saved everything of his. Old board games, golf clubs, even his favorite pair of argyle socks. She had to say goodbye to him, but she wouldn't give up the things that meant so much to him. I love to come up here and visit their memories."

Beau nodded because he couldn't think of anything appropriate to say. He picked up a tennis racket, then put it down—took a few steps and looked through a five-foot tower of pink plastic milk crates filled with record albums. Dean Martin, Johnny Mathis, Sam Cooke…somebody named Boxcar Willie. There was a turntable beside the plastic tower. "Does this record player still work?"

Smiling, Jenna crossed the floor to him, then pulled a folded extension cord down from one of the rafter braces. "What would you like to hear?"

He wanted to hear Sam Cooke, and he wasn't disappointed.

He was sitting on the floor with his back against the wall and his knees pulled up as "Twisting the Night

Away" ended and "Wonderful World" began. Then he had to say it. "I envy you this."

Jenna closed the lid on a new box of ornaments and sent him a soft look. "You envy me...the attic?"

"Yeah. There's so much family history here. I'll never have that. Anything that was important to my mother either left with her, or stayed behind for Jasper to sell."

She seemed to know that he didn't want her to ask questions or comment, and he appreciated it.

"We had this small china platter once. It was rectangular, about eight-by-twelve inches and was kind of translucent white. The edges were sort of ruffled." He studied his kneecaps. "There was a scene in the center of it—a meadow with pale green grass and pink wildflowers. It was the only material thing I ever felt an attachment to because my grandmother brought it with her from Ireland."

He looked up. "I'm not sure why I know that because Travis is French in origin. Maybe Jasper told me. Anyway, as heirlooms or family history goes, that was it. One day there was a link to the past, the next day it was gone."

Sam Cooke sang for a few minutes longer, then Beau rose to shut off the turntable and slide the record back in the album jacket. Jenna unplugged the extension cord and slung it back over the rafter brace. She didn't mention the story he'd shared until they were downstairs stringing white mini lights on the eight-foot tree. Then she stood back to assess their work and said casually, "Genealogy's a hobby of mine. If you want to trace your roots sometime, I'd love to help you." Then she handed him a crystal angel from a box and smiled. "I like to put these on the tree first. They're beautiful, aren't they?"

Beau felt his chest swell with so many emotions, he couldn't sort them all out. She knew he couldn't handle pity, so she'd kept any hint of sympathy from her voice. She'd just stated a fact and moved on.

Clearing his throat, he took the angel and reached high to hang it on a short branch near the top. Then he looked down at her and smiled. "Yeah," he said quietly. "Every angel in this room is beautiful."

Jenna rose on Wednesday morning feeling a warm glow. Though he hadn't said it, she sensed that Beau had never decorated a tree before, but she knew it had made him happy. And that made her happy. There'd been no reply to her offer to trace his roots, but that was okay. If he ever wanted to do it, she'd help him. There was a need in some people to know where they'd come from. Beau seemed to be one of them.

She got out of bed and started her day. The sun was shining, the sky was blue, and she and Beau would be leaving for Coudersport this afternoon. Today, she vowed to leave the wolf at the door, regain the mindset she'd adopted when he invited her to go geocaching, and have a good time.

It wasn't easy. Periodically, the doubts and fears crept back in, and she'd had to calm herself with prayer, logic and fact: Fish had provided a plausible reason for those hang-up calls, and "Mrs. Bolton," could have been acting alone for reasons known only to her. The funeral flowers had been more difficult to explain away. But as she and Beau had discussed, there *were* hackers who delighted in making trouble for people just because they could. She wanted desperately to believe that.

When they were in his truck and underway, Beau

glanced across at her and smiled at the way she was dressed. "I don't think I've seen you in jeans since we were in high school."

"When you live with a Victorian fashion plate who wears taffeta and lace most of the time, jeans seem a bit casual." But jeans, boots and a Dallas Cowboys sweatshirt suited Beau perfectly. His leather jacket lay in the backseat. Now, as they passed the busy Quick Mart, he turned down the volume on the country-rock music coming from his speakers. The song matched her new philosophy: "Live Like You Were Dying."

"Are you excited about the self-defense classes?"

"Yes, I'm really looking forward to them."

"Good. Fish thought it was a good idea, too."

Jenna glanced over at him. "You told Fish I was considering the classes?"

"It came up."

She suspected that a lot of things had come up while they'd talked yesterday. She unzipped the light blue parka she wore over her white sweater. The sun shining through the windows was heating up the cab. "I've been wondering about something."

"What's that?" He slowed at the intersection of Maine and Sassafras, then continued on.

"When Fish came to see you yesterday about the bullet holes in your sign, you said kids were probably to blame."

"Yes, I said that."

"But before you answered, there was a look that passed between you and Fish. What was that about?"

"A look?"

She sighed. "Beau, please. You know what I'm talking about. You don't believe it was kids. Why not?"

After a moment, he turned down the Tim McGraw

song, then trained his gaze on the road again. "Because the slugs Fish dug out of the wall behind my sign had some size to them. Kids don't usually carry nine-millimeter handguns."

A chill moved through her. "Who does?"

"Thugs, cops…someone with a grudge."

Jenna released an uneasy breath. He had someone in mind. She could hear it in his voice. "I imagine we can rule out the police," she said. "And I don't think Charity has a large contingent of thugs."

"Which we can be thankful for."

"Yes. That leaves someone with a grudge. Who?"

"When Fish asked if I'd ticked off anyone lately, the only person I could think of was Frank Killian."

"Frank?" she repeated. "You and Frank are having problems?"

"No. Actually, we get along. At least we did. But that look he gave us after church on Sunday could've curdled milk. Maybe he resents my replacing him at the Blackberry."

"Even if he does, I can't see him shooting at your shop. He's an intelligent man. Besides, if he wanted to retaliate, I'm a more logical candidate. I fired him." The connection he'd apparently wanted her to make hit her hard and Jenna released a soft "Oh." She shifted on the bench seat to face him. "Fish thinks Frank's responsible for the bullet holes and the vandalism at the inn?"

"No, he's saying it's a possibility. I phoned him a while ago. He tried to see Killian yesterday, but apparently, he's out of town."

Jenna shook her head. It wasn't Frank. "Hiring someone to vandalize the inn would require money, and he's having financial problems."

"Maybe he had a friend who was willing to help for free."

"If that's so, he would've needed a friend with some serious skills. Someone who could hack into my pass-word-protected computer. My credit card, too, if every-thing is connected."

"Do you know what Frank's sister does for a living?"

Knowing he wouldn't have asked if the answer wasn't relevant, Jenna hesitated. "I thought Barbara managed the cell phone store in the mall."

"She does. But she also has a successful side busi-ness building and repairing computers. If Frank needed a loan, he might've gotten it from the Bank of Barbara."

Ahead on the right, two flags snapped in the wind near a white-sided convenience store—the Stars and Stripes in the superior position, and an NFL banner be-neath it. Beau flicked on his turn signal, pulled off the road and coasted to the pumps. He shut off the truck and released his seat belt. "Give me a minute to fill the tank, then we can head inside for coffee or a soft drink. We still have an hour of road time left."

Jenna was barely aware of him outside. Suddenly the chance that Frank and Barbara Killian were to blame was almost calming because they were basically good people who wouldn't take this any further. This could be over! She wouldn't even press charges. She'd just count her blessings and go back to living without fear. At least in the immediate present.

She was still feeling relatively good about that two and a half hours later when they left the Haskells and started for home. Snow fell, accumulating on the berms where the salt trucks couldn't reach. Warm air from the vents melted big, fluffy flurries as soon as they hit the windshield.

"I enjoyed meeting the Haskells," she said. "They seem really happy together, don't they?"

"Yeah, they do." Beau flicked on his wipers. "I hope they stay that way."

"Why wouldn't they?"

He shrugged. "People change. Sometimes things that make them happy at first, aren't quite good enough later on."

"Like what?"

"I don't know. Things."

Obviously, he wasn't talking about the Haskells now. But respecting his privacy and realizing how difficult it was for him to share personal information, Jenna remained silent.

Beau nodded through the windshield. "There's a little place a few miles up the road that's geared to kids, but the food's good. When's the last time you had a great bowl of chili?"

"Never?"

"Then you're in for a treat."

Auntie Em's Diner was a shiny silver-and-chrome throwback to the fifties, but inside, it was what people expected. Laminated playbills hung in the windows, while *Wizard of Oz* character figures occupied every available surface that wasn't needed for food preparation or dining. The ceiling was a glossy, hand-painted poppy field, the brilliant red repeated in the vinyl-covered booths. Behind the lunch counter hung a framed photo of an older woman holding a darling little toddler in a blue-and-white-checked pinafore.

They were enjoying their hot rolls and cheddar-and-green onion-topped chili, when out of the blue, Beau said, "I wasn't talking about the Haskells back there."

Jenna put down her spoon and spoke quietly. "I know."

"That's what I thought." Then without fanfare or explanation, he began. "I met Shelley when I was stationed at Fort Dix. I'm not sure if I cared about her because I wanted the family, marriage and kids thing that I'd never had, or if my feelings for her were legitimate." He blew out a dry laugh. "Not that I was prepared for any of it. I was a little short on role models growing up."

"Were you afraid you wouldn't be good at it?"

"I don't know. Maybe. Obviously, Shelley and I didn't work out. She was an officer's daughter who liked the idea of moving around—seeing new places. I wanted stability."

He reached for the jar of crushed red pepper flakes beside the napkin dispenser and added a dash to his bowl. "Beth came along after I'd finished trade school and was apprenticing in New Jersey. Under normal circumstances we would've never met. We were poles apart. But she blew a tire one night on the Jersey Turnpike, and when she swerved to the side of the road and hit her emergency flashers, I pulled in behind her."

"How long were you together?"

"Almost a year if you count continuous days. Less than three months of actual time. She worked for a pharmaceuticals corporation, so she was gone a lot. I'm not sure why it lasted as long as it did, except that she was beautiful and intelligent and when we were alone, it worked. But when her friends showed up or she entertained people in the medical community, the champagne flutes and designer wardrobe came out, and her vocabulary shot up six notches." He stirred his chili. "Then one day she suggested—very kindly—that

I needed to go back to school because I was capable of doing a lot more than swinging a hammer."

For a second, Jenna was utterly speechless. "She said that?"

"Not exactly, but that was the gist of it. So I told her I already had a trade and called it quits. I knew what she meant. I didn't fit in her world, and she didn't want to live in mine."

Beau paused, met her eyes, then brought them full circle. He wasn't sure why he'd spilled his guts like that. Maybe because he'd already opened a door by telling her about that china platter. Either that, or part of him wanted her to know that his love life hadn't been a walk in the park, either. "Anyway, that's what I meant about some things only pleasing people in the short term."

Her smile went straight to his heart. "Know what?"

He shook his head.

"For an intelligent woman, she wasn't very smart."

He begged to differ. "Actually, she was. She realized long before I did that it wasn't going to work. She gave me the honor of bailing out before she had to."

"Not the way I see it. Do you believe our lives are preordained? That God sets us on a course, and there's no changing it?"

"I hadn't really thought about it. What do you believe?"

"I believe that we're exactly where we're supposed to be at this moment. I think that the things we endure make us stronger, and when an opportunity for happiness presents itself, we should say yes. Beth made a mistake." She held his gaze. "And I'm glad she did, for two very selfish reasons. If you were in New Jersey with her, I wouldn't be enjoying this bowl of chili, and

I wouldn't have the best carpenter in the state working on my inn."

"Yeah?"

Her smile softened. "Yeah."

Something meaningful passed between them, something that was more than empathy, more than admiration. Something that seemed to quiet the music on the jukebox and create an airy feeling in Beau's chest. And from the suddenly self-conscious look on her face he knew Jenna had felt it, too.

By the time they reached the Blackberry and he'd parked in the small lot, their snowy world was a Courier and Ives wonderland—and Beau was still trying to decide what to do about that moment at the diner. They'd continued to talk as though nothing had changed, but there was a nerve-tingling, underlying awareness between them that assured him that something had.

Shrugging into his jacket, he got out, then rounded the truck to open Jenna's door. She'd already stepped down. Light from the windows and landscaping spangled every snow-covered tree and shrub, glistened on the walkway.

"Quite a change since we left this afternoon," he said quietly as they followed the path to the security pad near the side door.

Her voice sounded hollow in the night's stillness. "Chances are, most of it will be gone tomorrow since daytime temperatures are supposed to stay in the forties all week."

Jenna tapped in the day's security code, then turned around to meet his eyes. Her smile faltered. Snowflakes fell softly around them, and their warm breath fogged the air. Somewhere in the back of his mind, a voice whispered that doing what he was thinking could be a mistake. But it was hard to hear over the thudding pulse in his ears. Beau touched her face, slid a hand under her silky blond hair to bring her close. Then before common sense could intervene, he bent to cover her lips with his own.

NINE

Jenna leaned into him as Beau's lips moved softly over hers, then lingered for a few seconds of sweet exploration before he eased away. For a time, she simply floated on the moment. Then she slowly opened her eyes and watched big white snowflakes gather in his dark hair and coat the shoulders of his leather jacket.

The door behind them flew open. "Inside! Both of you!" Aunt Molly said sharply. "Hurry."

Startled, they exchanged a quick, what's-going-on look, then did as she asked and shut the door behind them. Molly stood clutching the front of her long pink chenille robe.

"Aunt Molly, what's wrong?"

"More hang-up calls—three in a row. And this time I heard someone breathing on the line before he broke the connection."

"Okay," Jenna said tensely. "Business or no business, we're having the Blackberry's number changed."

Beau spoke. "Did you call Fish?"

"Yes, but he wasn't on duty. Chief Baboon was." They followed her into the kitchen where the table in the nook was set for the three of them. "He said he'd look into it."

Beau pulled out a chair, but apparently too wired to sit, Molly waved away the offer. "He checked our caller ID history, but the number was blocked. He said he'll know more after he gets our phone company records."

"So he *is* going to check with the phone company. Good."

Molly nodded. "He also said that disposable phones are hard to trace, and if the person who called was smart, that phone's already at the bottom of a river."

Jenna gave her great aunt a squeeze, then released her. She didn't like seeing her like this. Without the high button shoes that gave her height, and the velveteen, knitted shawls and lace that gave her bulk, she felt like a bony baby bird. "I'm so sorry this happened. Why didn't you call my cell?"

"I didn't want to ruin your evening." Despite her distress, she managed a smile. "And from what I saw outside, it went very well."

A pleasant shiver moved through her, but Jenna couldn't think about that kiss right now.

Molly's feisty spirit came roaring back. "Just so you know, I wasn't afraid for myself. I was afraid for the two of you. That's why I called you inside. I didn't want you standing out there under the light in case some kook decided to—" Halting abruptly, she drew a breath and pulled herself up to her full four foot ten. "I'm not going to Hartford."

Jenna spoke firmly. "You have to go. Now more than ever. If there's something nasty on the horizon, I'll feel better knowing that you're safe."

"And how am *I* going to feel if you need me, and I'm celebrating with Millie in New England?"

Beau moved to her side. "Aunt Molly, there are two things that you need to remember. I hate to sound like

Perris, but the first thing is, there've been no outward threats on Jenna's life. If the hang-ups are connected to the vandalism and credit card fraud, it's still basically harassment and destruction of property. The second thing is, while you're away—with the exception of grabbing a shower at my place sometime during the day—I'll be here. No one's going to bother her. Now, please. Don't change your plans."

When her aunt had finally capitulated and gone upstairs to bed, Jenna prowled the breakfast nook where Aunt Molly had set out a few fresh apple-crumb muffins and a carafe of decaf coffee. She couldn't eat or drink a thing. Apparently, Beau couldn't, either.

"Think we should wrap the muffins up so they don't dry out?" he asked, carrying them to the work island.

Nodding, Jenna opened a drawer and without conscious direction, removed a roll of plastic wrap, then covered the platter. Ever since Aunt Molly had gone upstairs, she'd been reliving the conversation she'd had with Detective Caspian. She looked at Beau. "Do you watch much TV? Other than football and the news magazine show you called about last week?"

"Some," he replied. "Why?"

"Have you ever seen a program on police profilers?"

"Yes. Again, why?"

"Because when I spoke to the detective on my case a few days ago, he asked if Courtland had been on my mind because the two-year anniversary of my attack was approaching. At the time, I thought that he might've had a point—that maybe the date had been drifting in my subconscious for a while and I'd been overreacting to the things that happened."

Beau waited through her pause.

"The FBI agent I saw on TV mentioned something

similar about a serial killer who'd been inactive for a long time, then suddenly began killing again. The agent—profiler—suspected that something had happened in the man's life to make him kill again. He called it a 'stressor.'" She swallowed. "The day I found out about the identity theft, Aunt Molly asked why Courtland would wait two years to torment me. Maybe the anniversary of my attack was his stressor."

"Jenna—"

"I know," she said wearily. "Analyzing isn't doing me any good. It's just that I don't think Perris is taking this seriously enough."

"You could be right. But you also need to look at this from his perspective. In Pennsylvania, simple harassment is either a summary offense or a third-degree misdemeanor. On average, the punishment's a fine and up to a year in jail, depending on the judge who rules. Perris will do what's required—but probably not much more."

"You reeled off that information pretty quickly. It came from Fish, didn't it?"

"No, it came from the internet, and the rationale about Perris's handling of the case is all mine. It's just a hunch." He sent her a grim look. "Then again, there's a lot to be said for gut-level hunches like yours."

She felt some hope. "You believe Courtland's behind this, too?"

"I didn't say that. But you believe it, and it's scaring you. That's why I'm bunking on your couch tonight. That is," he added, "if it's okay with you."

Jenna nodded. "It's more than okay." She wasn't only worried about herself now, she was worried about Aunt Molly.

"All right, then. In the morning, I'll pick up the

sander and whatever else I'll need to refinish the floor, then head to my place to clean up, pack a few things and hitch up my camper. I meant what I told Aunt Molly. I'll be here until you throw me out, or until you feel secure again."

Secure? She couldn't recall the last time she felt secure. No…no, that wasn't true. She was beginning to feel secure right now. "Thank you, but if you're sleeping on the couch tonight, there's no reason to bring your camper over tomorrow."

Beau shook his head. "There's every reason. Aunt Molly's here tonight. On Friday, she'll be gone. We both know how gossip spreads in this town."

"I don't care about gossip."

"But I do. I don't want your neighbors to talk."

In the end, Beau's height resulted in a change in sleeping arrangements. The sofas in the parlor were too short to accommodate him, so despite his insistence that he didn't need to stretch out, Jenna did some pressuring of her own and sent him to one of the guest rooms.

Now, with everyone settled in their rooms, she pulled her Bible from her nightstand and tried to read. It didn't take long for her to realize she couldn't concentrate on scripture until she asked God for help. "So what do I do about this, Lord?" she murmured. "I'm attracted to him, and if I read his reaction at Auntie Em's tonight, he feels something for me. But what if getting close to me puts him at risk?" Court's reaction to her hugging Malcolm had been so over-the-top, she'd often wondered if he would've hurt Mal, too, given the chance.

She pressed a hand to her abdomen, visualizing the scars beneath her nightgown. "Aunt Molly will be safe in Connecticut, but Beau will be here, and he's becoming more important to me every day. I couldn't live with myself if something happened to him." Because aside from the fear that had become her constant companion, the only thing she knew for sure was this: Whenever she relived that kiss, she felt a sweet, wonderful breathlessness. She wanted them both to live long enough to see what happened next.

She was lost in the crippling fog, running, running—hearing rapid footsteps behind her. He was coming for her again! She darted across the road to the next street, only to find that she was back where she started. And he was there again, the knife flashing under the glow of a streetlight that seemed to move with him. She cried out—kept running. But something was wrong. How could she see behind her when she was facing forward? Yet she could, and there was blood on the blade! But he hadn't reached her yet, had he? She stopped—pressed her hands to her stomach—felt the soft, warm wetness there. And a scream tore from her throat.

"Jenny! Jenny, wake up!"

Jenna vaulted to a seated position on the bed, her breaths coming in short gulps, her heart racing like a runaway train. She looked around, tried to focus. Tried to get her bearings.

"It's all right. You're safe. You're here with me. Tell me you know you're okay."

Her voice shook so badly Jenna barely recognized it as her own. "Yes. Y-yes, I know." There was no fog, no man with a knife. No blood. There was only soft lamplight, and Aunt Molly sitting on the side of her bed, looking incredibly worried. "I'm so sorry."

Her aunt's smile made her feel even worse. "For what?"

"For waking you. Dear God. Did you hear me all the way upstairs? Did *he?*"

"I don't think so, or he'd be standing in the doorway. I wouldn't have heard you, either, if I hadn't come down to the kitchen for a glass of milk."

"You couldn't sleep?"

Molly turned the clock on the nightstand so Jenna could see it. "It's not even eleven yet. I wanted to catch the late news. Was it the same dream?"

She nodded. "Promise me something?"

"You don't want Beau to know."

"Yes. Please don't tell him."

"I won't," she said gently. "Can you sleep now? Or would you like to stay up and watch the news with me?" She summoned a smile. "I'll even share my milk with you."

How blessed she was to have such a loving angel in her corner. How very blessed. Smiling, Jenna took the TV's remote from the nightstand, then shifted over so her skinny little protector could join her. She hit the power button and the small TV set on her dresser flickered to life. "You're here now," she said. "Why don't you watch the news with me?"

Early the next morning, Beau unlocked the door to his house, flicked on the kitchen light, then dropped his keys and yesterday's mail on the table. Crossing to the counter, he poured leftover coffee into a mug and stuck it in the microwave. Jenna and Aunt Molly had wanted him to stay for breakfast, but he'd begged off, saying he needed to get an early start staining the trim stacked in his truck. What he'd actually needed was some time alone.

What a night. And he wasn't only referring to Jenna's fear of being stalked. He was afraid he'd started something he couldn't—or shouldn't—finish.

It was only a kiss, he told himself. Not a lifetime commitment. So why did he keep reliving it?

You know why, a disparaging voice said from the back of his mind. *Kissing her meant something.*

Yes, it had. Absurd as it sounded, a radiating sense of rightness had spread through him when their lips touched and their warm breaths mingled. He'd never felt anything close to that with any other woman. And he'd liked it.

The microwave beeped. Retrieving his coffee, he carried it to the table and sorted through his mail. At the diner she'd asked if he thought he wouldn't be good at marriage and parenting because of his upbringing. Good question. He'd been abandoned by both parents, raised in squalor by a grandfather who'd never had a kind word for him, and he'd hung out with teenage hoods. Nothing about his life made him a suitable match for her. Not for Webb Harper's pretty princess. He wondered if Harper had told Jenna about his years-ago conversation with Aunt Molly. Had he quoted statistics? Pointed out that children who'd been emotionally abused often *became* abusers? That was something Beau still couldn't wrap his mind around. He'd never treat a child the way Jasper had treated him—not on the worst day of his life.

And why was he even thinking about things that smacked of a future with Jenna? She was a friend and, at the moment, his employer. That's all.

He took a sip of coffee, grimaced, and dumped it in

the sink. Maybe the best thing for him to do was watch over her from a distance and leave the rest of it alone.

If he could.

The day flew by. Beau picked up the sander, stained more trim and fixed the catch on Aunt Molly's dated suitcase. Then, around noon, he and Jenna treated her to a pre-birthday celebration at the diner. A quick phone call to the bakery this morning had resulted in a huge, decorated sheet cake being carried into the diner just as they'd finished eating. He'd never seen Molly smile as brightly, especially when the entire lunch crowd started singing "Happy Birthday." She'd insisted on taking cake around to everyone there. Now, the birthday girl was meeting with her faith-sharing group, and he and Jenna were entering the Charity Youth and Community center for her first self-defense class.

Located in the middle of town on an offshoot of Main Street, it was a long, one-story yellow brick building with a brown hip roof, and sat just beyond the police department's doors. Rumor had it that, decades ago, the stuffy town fathers had specifically chosen that spot after their first terrifying glimpse of rock and roll. If there was any rowdy behavior, they'd said, it was only a hundred yards to the nearest jail cell.

"Well," Beau said as they approached one of the larger meeting rooms and Jenna slipped off her jacket. "This is where we part company. Have fun." He had to smile. She looked young, trim and pretty in her ponytail, soft purple tracksuit and white T-shirt.

"I'll do my best. You're not going to hang around and check out the class?"

"Nope, I'm going to find a chair, then read for a while." He pulled a paperback out of his jacket pocket—

Michael Connelly's *The Lincoln Lawyer.* "Then again, this is a three-hour class. If I get tired of sitting, I'll be back."

"Great. And Beau?" Her features softened. "Thank you."

He waved off her thanks. "I'll see you in a little while."

The twenty folding chairs in the room were arranged in a semicircle, with one chair in front, presumably for the instructor. Behind them, thick gray gymnastics mats that might've come from the high school lay end to end on the hardwood floor.

Many of the chairs were already filled, so Jenna took a seat next to cute little brunette Mitzi Abbott, who was one of the younger waitresses at the diner. They talked about Mitzi's college choices for a while, and how she'd feel about leaving slow-moving Charity for a city environment. Then Mitzi glanced around at the rest of their chattering classmates and dropped her voice.

"Can I ask you something?" She went on before Jenna could reply. "This afternoon, when I was helping you folks take Mrs. Jennings's birthday cake around to customers, one of the other waitresses—well, it was Patty Lorrigan—said you and Beau came in for lunch last week, too. So are you guys a couple now? I mean, I don't want to be nosy, but..." She laughed. "Inquiring minds want to know."

"We're friends," Jenna answered. "Just friends."

She looked genuinely disappointed. "Really? Because Patty said—"

She was saved from hearing what else Patty said when their slender, redheaded instructor came into the room.

"Okay, everyone," Megan Carlyle said after she'd introduced herself as a former mugging victim. "Before we get into self-defense techniques, I'd like to devote a little time to the dos and don'ts of staying safe." She passed out folders to each of the attendees. "Inside, you'll find a list of tips that could keep you from becoming a victim, but we'll discuss a few of them, anyway." She looked concerned. "I understand there was a serial killer operating here a while ago, so many of you will find the advice familiar."

After practicing extreme caution for two years, Jenna knew those dos and don'ts better than most people. Additionally, one of her two best friends had been immersed in the Gold Star Killer case. Margo McBride Blackburn had been chief of police at the time.

"Okay, first and foremost," Carlyle said. "Always walk in well-lit areas, and stay away from bushes, recessed doorways and other dark, potential hiding places. The night I was mugged, I was in a hurry to get home to watch my favorite TV show, so I took a shortcut through a park that was fairly well lit. Unfortunately, it was also beautifully landscaped. I ended up in the hospital for five days, and the dental bill for my four capped teeth was astronomical. All for a TV show." She grinned wryly. "So please, be smarter about your safety than I was."

The lecture part of the class went on for another half hour, then they chose partners, and the defense techniques portion began. Jenna turned around when their instructor flashed a smile at someone in the back of the classroom—then felt her skin warm as Carlyle beckoned Beau forward.

"Since everyone has a partner but me, I wonder if you'd like to help me out this evening, Mister—?"

"Travis," he said, coming forward. "Sure. What would you like me to do?"

She laughed. "You can strangle me. Gently."

Sending Jenna a grin, he moved to the front of the room where Carlyle took his hands and placed them on her throat. She turned to the class. "Okay, now there are several things you can do in a situation like this, but let's start with the simplest. Instinctively, you'll try to pry your attacker's hands away, but that's not easy to do. Your best bet is to inflict some pain." Reaching up, she peeled Beau's little finger away from her throat and gave it a jerk. He winced.

"Yank that little digit back as hard as you can—break it if you can. Your attacker can't help but loosen his grip. That will give you one, maybe two seconds to grab his shirt and land three hard knee pumps where they'll do the most good. Then *run*."

Soft laughter rolled through the class at Beau's beleaguered look.

"That's the purpose of this class," Carlyle went on sincerely. "To give you time to save yourself. Unless a woman is extremely strong or a trained fighter, she's not going to win the battle with a man who's intent upon doing her harm." She looked around, her gaze resting on each of them. "Remember what I said earlier. Adrenaline can make you freeze. You need to make it work *for* you, not against you."

She smiled at Beau. "Thank you, Mr. Travis. Now if you'd like to stick around and be our guinea pig for a while, we'd love to have you."

With a doubtful look and a chuckle, he shook his head. "Thanks, but if it's okay with you, I'll just hang out in the back of the room and watch."

When the class ended at nine, Jenna said goodbye

to her friends, thanked the instructor for an informative session, then walked back to meet Beau, who was holding her jacket. He helped her slip it on, then flipped up her collar. Tiny nerve endings reacted to his touch.

"So what did you think?" she asked as they headed for the door.

He gave her a lopsided grin. "I think I'd think twice before tangling with your instructor. She's lethal. And she's right about the need to practice those defensive moves again and again—the way martial arts students do." His brow lined. "God willing, you'll never have to use what you learned tonight. But if the situation arises—and fear shuts down your mind—those automatic body responses could save your life."

"I know. I wish I'd taken this course two years ago."

"Same here." He ushered her into the brisk night air, then halted abruptly when a gray van bearing a dry cleaner's name and logo shot past them and sailed into the street. Beau shook his head in disdain, then they continued across the lot to his running truck. "Did you tell Ms. Carlyle that you might be a little late for class tomorrow?"

"Yes. She was fine with it. Hopefully Aunt Molly's flight will leave on schedule and I'll—we'll—get here on time."

"Then you're enjoying it?"

"Yes, it's great." Laughing, she quoted an old Helen Reddy song. "'I am woman. Hear me roar.'"

They were about to leave the lot when a Charity PD cruiser rolled up beside them and Fish lowered his window. Beau did the same.

"Glad I caught you before you left," Fish called. "I just came from the Blackberry. Ms. Jennings said you'd be here."

"Something going on, Fish?"

"Nothing new. I just wanted to tell you that I spoke to Frank Killian. He wasn't real happy with my questions, but he'll get over it. Anyway, he's got a handgun, but it's a little .22, not a nine mil."

"No offense," Beau said, "and I'm not telling you how to do your job. But did you look for other weapons, or just take him at his word?"

With an uncomfortable look, he waved off Beau's concerns. "I don't think he shot up your sign, Beau. Frank even offered to take a polygraph—which are a lot more accurate these days."

Jenna saw Beau frown and imagined what he was thinking. "A lot more accurate" still left room for error.

"What about the trouble at the Blackberry?"

Fish shifted his attention to her. "Sorry, Jenna. Nothing on the BOLO yet. We're still working on your hang-ups." He let his wheels roll slowly as she and Beau both offered their thanks. "Just doing my job," he said with a grin and a wave. "I'll talk to you, soon."

Aunt Molly had warm spinach balls and cream puffs waiting for them when they returned to the Blackberry—leftovers from her faith sharing meeting. Once Beau was seated with a cup of green tea—which he only accepted out of courtesy—she stared directly into his eyes.

"Jenna tells me you're still planning to sleep in your camper while I'm gone."

"Yes, I'll bring it over tomorrow and park it near the side door. That way, if I have to leave for a while during the day to pick up something, it'll still give the appearance that someone's here with her."

Molly put down her teacup and harrumphed. "That's

the most preposterous thing I've ever heard. This home has two suites and four bedrooms with private baths. The idea of you sleeping in a tin box without an electric and water hook-up is utter nonsense. I want you to stay here at the inn."

Beau shook his head. "I can't. Jenna doesn't need any grief from the rumor mill. And believe me, she'd get plenty."

Molly's determined look remained. "I admire your chivalry, but I believe I misspoke. If you don't do as I ask, I'm not leaving. While you're snoring away in that tuna can of yours, someone could sneak past you and get to my girl. I want you inside. As for people talking… My late husband had a saying. 'If they're talking about me, they're leaving someone else alone.' Jenny and I feel the same." Smiling, she patted his hand. "Now why don't you finish your tea, then go back to your house and pack?"

"Aunt Molly," Beau said in exasperation. "It's not going to happ—"

The phone rang. Leaving the two of them to argue, Jenna went to the foyer to answer it. The voice on the line was warm, friendly and feminine, and it belonged to Revered Landers's wife.

"Jenna, it's Miriam Landers. Please forgive me for calling so late."

"Not a problem, Miriam. We're still up. How are you?"

"Fine, but I'm afraid I'm in need of a huge favor."

"Of course. Just name it."

"Is there any chance you have a room available for the next few days? My cousin Bernice is coming in for mine and Paul's fiftieth wedding anniversary dinner and staying through Thanksgiving Day. With everyone else here for the celebration and the holiday, our home—and our daughter's—is practically bursting at the seams. Originally, Bernice said she couldn't make it. Then she called a few minutes ago and said her plans had suddenly changed. She's driving up from Lancaster tomorrow."

Jenna winced. Of all people to have to turn away. "I'm so sorry. The inn is closed until Christmas week. Beau Travis is doing some carpentry work for us." She didn't see any need to mention ants or razor blades. "Have you tried the Tall Spruce?"

"No, but our son did, and they're full. Bernice just needs a place to sleep, Jenna. She wouldn't even need breakfast because she'll be eating here with the rest of us. And I'm sure Beau won't be hammering all night."

"No, but—"

Gentle steamroller that she was, Miriam pressed on. "Are you sure there's nothing you can do for us? Bernice introduced me to Paul. I'm afraid there wouldn't be a fiftieth anniversary to celebrate if it hadn't been for her."

Jenna hid a sigh. It was time to come clean. "Miriam, I'd let her have a room free of charge if there wasn't another problem. A few days ago we found some ants in the kitchen. We believe they're just a bad memory now, but I can't be positive. I wouldn't want your cousin to be upset if she encountered—"

Miriam laughed softly. "Bernice lives on a farm. Believe me, a few ants won't put her off in the least. Thank you and God bless you, honey. She won't be any trouble at all."

Aunt Molly was still browbeating Beau when Jenna reentered the room. "Well, the problem's solved," she said to the two of them. "I just booked a guest through Thanksgiving Day."

"You booked a guest?" Molly repeated, startled.

Jenna nodded. "Free of charge."

When she finished explaining about Bernice Gates's sudden need for a room, Molly chuckled softly. "You say her plans changed suddenly?"

"Only moments ago, according to Miriam."

Aunt Molly beamed. "Well, now. It seems the Lord wants me to go to Connecticut." She winked at Beau. "And He apparently wants you to sleep in a decent bed."

It was nearly eleven when Beau said good-night and carried his duffel bag upstairs to the room he'd used the night before. Closing the door, he tossed his pack on the Rose Room's sky-high faux featherbed. He still felt uneasy about staying inside—but not for himself. He'd gotten used to gossip a long time ago. He just didn't want Jenna's name on every rumor-mongering tongue in town. He glanced skyward. "Take care of that, will You?" he whispered.

Jenna crossed her dark room to the window looking out on the lighted gazebo and stared at the glistening snow. Beau had been wonderful tonight, getting all strong and protective when he saw the vehicle tracks leading up the inclined drive to the Blackberry, then telling her to sit tight until he checked things out. There'd been nothing to worry about. One set of tracks had belonged to Fish, which they'd known. The other set was Elmer Fox's. Elmer had stopped by with a few of those promised daguerreotypes. As soon as Bertie at the historical society picked the prints she wanted, he'd be dropping off a few more.

Now as Jenna looked out on the still night, something she'd been denying for days settled in with a mixture of happiness and uneasiness. She'd fallen in love with Beau, and she was fairly certain he cared about her, too. Maybe it wasn't love…but it could be.

"He's the one, Lord," she murmured. "But there are so many reasons I shouldn't let myself hope for a life with him." Only one of those reasons weighed heavily on her mind tonight, however. "He deserves everything wonderful life has to offer. A real home and a loving family. But even if You see fit to take away the fear in my life, and somehow he does want to be with me…" She swallowed. "What if I can't give him a child?"

Because of construction traffic they arrived at the small Dubois Regional Airport a little later than they'd planned, but still made it with a half hour to spare. Jenna smiled as Beau lifted Aunt Molly down from the front seat, then took Jenna's hand, too, though they both knew she didn't need any help. Minutes later, they'd crossed the lot to the buff-colored brick terminal and joined other commuters in the airport's restaurant.

It had been a busy morning. Miriam Landers's cousin Bernice had arrived shortly before lunchtime, and with a bright smile, she'd exclaimed that the small turret room would do beautifully for her. She'd also reiterated that she wouldn't be needing breakfast. Jenna assured her that she was welcome to change her mind anytime and hoped that Bernice's presence would finally put Beau's "gossip" reservations to rest.

The flight deck was an open, high-ceilinged affair with an L-shaped lunch counter and some nice aeronautical touches—like the airplane mobiles suspended from the ceiling, and the historical photographs on the wall.

Settling at a table, they ordered hot drinks, then talked about the sitting room's restoration and Jenna's self-defense classes. Aunt Molly alone brought up the elephant in the room. Strangely, though, her tone was almost cheerful.

"Now if anything happens while I'm gone, I expect a phone call. I don't want to be 'out of the loop,' as folks say nowadays."

Jenna shook her head. The last thing she'd do if "anything happened" was call and ruin her aunt's vacation. "Nothing's going to happen."

"You never know about these things," Aunt Molly replied, a baffling twinkle in her eyes. "Emma Lucille could finally get through 'Amazing Grace' without hitting the wrong keys or Elmer Fox could win the lottery." She pushed her teacup away. "A nice-looking couple might even wake up one morning and see that they're perfect for each other. Why, by the time I get back, they might even be engaged."

Mortified, Jenna prayed for the floor to swallow her up.

Beau simply gestured through the plate glass wall at an approaching private plane. Though sunset was still a good half hour away and cloud cover was minimal, the afternoon light was fading. "Fine-looking plane out there on the runway, isn't it?"

Aunt Molly sighed. "All right. A house doesn't have to fall on me. I'll behave." She turned to Jenna. "Now, promise me you'll phone if anything out of the ordinary happens, because I can come back home immediately. Millie will understand."

"I'll be fine," she said. "Just have a good time, and don't worry."

"I'll try not to. Oh—and don't forget the Fruitcake Fling tomorrow afternoon. It starts at one o'clock."

"I won't."

Forty-five minutes later, Aunt Molly was well on her way, and Jenna and Beau were driving toward the community center and Jenna's second class. Though neither of them had mentioned Aunt Molly's outrageous words in the airport restaurant, it still bothered her. "Sorry about that thing at the airport."

"What thing?"

"The engagement thing. Aunt Molly believes that with age comes the privilege of saying whatever she wants, whenever she wants."

"She's been good to me," he returned, pulling into the center's crowded lot and easing the truck into a parking space. "She can say whatever she likes."

"Good. I'm glad you weren't offended."

He shut off the truck. "Offended? I was flattered that she'd even think that was possible. Now," he said, turning to her. "Are you ready to kick some booty?"

He was flattered? That joyful feeling ballooned in her chest again and Jenna smiled. "You bet I am."

He roamed the room, turning the diamond stud in his ear as yesterday's recording played. Her aunt would be gone for five days, and soon the carpenter would be gone, too, further isolating her. She wouldn't keep Travis around long after that other piece of… for lack of a better word, *evidence*…showed up. And what was taking them so long to find it?"

Pausing the recording, he took the disposable cell phone from the desk and called one of the two numbers programmed into it. They were new numbers, the old phones they'd purchased in Ohio, now useless. Thug One answered.

"Where's your friend?"

"In the van. Listening."

"Tell him I'm still not pleased with the clarity of those songs he downloaded for me. Can anything be done about that?"

"Not unless we want to be noticed."

He scowled. "Then continue as before."

"Like your new digs?"

"Not particularly." But there were no four-star hotels this far from Pittsburgh. "Are you tracking delivery on the package?"

"It should reach her in a day or two."

"Good." He broke the connection. Naturally, she would call the police when it arrived—and they would do nothing. Because there was nothing they *could* do.

TEN

Saturday morning dawned bright and beautiful, with a golden sun trying its best to melt the thin layer of snow still covering the lawns and frosting the trees. The Chamber would have a good day for the Fruit-cake Fling. Jenna had been up since six-thirty brewing coffee, arranging fruit in bowls and cutting thick slabs of bread for French toast. Bernice Gates had popped in at seven-twenty to thank her again for the room, then hurried off to join the Landerses.

At seven-forty-five Beau came downstairs. The jitters she'd been feeling all morning multiplied. He looked rugged and outdoorsy. His dark hair was damp from his shower, and a blue plaid flannel shirt hung open over his black T-shirt.

"Good morning," she said. "How did you sleep?"

He grinned. "I'd say 'like a baby,' but babies aren't the best sleepers, are they?"

She smiled. "I couldn't say."

"Well, hopefully we'll both know the answer one day."

Jenna felt a pinch, but maintained her smile. "I just started the French toast. It'll be done in a minute. In the meantime, help yourself to coffee, fruit and muffins over there in the nook."

He didn't have to be asked twice. "You shouldn't have gone to so much trouble. I don't eat breakfast, remember?"

Yes, she remembered. She remembered everything about him, especially the kiss that had taken her breath away. She just hoped the kiss was the result of honest feelings, not an automatic reaction because he'd walked her to her door.

Beau picked up the carafe and filled their coffee cups. "Did Aunt Molly call last night?"

"Yes, as soon as she got in." Jenna flipped their French toast, then carried warm syrup from the microwave to the table. "She knew I'd worry if she didn't. She was tired, but glad to see Millie."

"Speaking of worrying," he said as she returned to the range. "I planned to move the furniture out of the sitting room first thing this morning, but when I accessed my phone messages, there was a call from Aggie Benson. She has a leak under her sink, and can't reach a plumber. She said it's not an emergency, but if you don't object, I'd like to check it out for her."

"How could I object after she okayed our bringing a cake into the diner? I doubt many restaurant owners would've done that."

"Not owners who count on selling desserts to their customers, for sure." He ambled over to her—watched her dust their French toast with confectioners sugar and add a garnish of fresh strawberries and orange slices. He carried their plates to the table. "You should probably go with me. Aunt Molly will have my head if I leave you alone."

Jenna felt her buoyant mood sink a little. She

would've preferred that he didn't qualify the invitation, but going was out of the question anyway. He pulled out her chair, and smiling her thanks, she sat. "Sorry, but today's the Chamber's fundraiser. I need to have the extra fruitcakes there by one o'clock."

"I know. I'm taking you. We'll be finished long before one." Dropping into the seat across from her, he nodded at the box of wrapped fruitcakes on the work island. "It looks like the work's done, so you have time, right? What do you say?"

Despite the backhanded invitation, Jenna's heart did a silly little stutter step. How could she say no when every square inch of her wanted to spend as much time with him as she could? "I say yes."

"Good." He scanned the table, his warm gaze taking in their place settings, the crock of strawberry jam, the whipping-cream-topped fruit and the stack of French toast on his plate. "If this tastes as good as it looks and smells, I might have to pay Aunt Molly to stay a few extra days. Thank you."

That sweet airy feeling returned. "You're welcome. Now let's ask the Blessing and dig in."

Aggie Benson was delighted to see them when they stopped at the busy diner for the key to her house. She'd been doing her own home improvements since her husband passed away several years ago, but her attempt at installing two shutoff valves under her sink had failed. She wrapped Beau in a bear hug.

"Food or fee?" she asked, chuckling.

"Food," he answered. "Always."

"Great. Dinner's on the house this week. Anything on the menu." Aggie grinned at Jenna. "Dinner for two."

It didn't take long to fix the leak, but as they'd crouched on the floor and Jenna handed Beau the tools he needed, it brought back memories for Jenna—nice memories of her mom and dad doing the same thing. It felt so right, she couldn't stop herself from wondering "what if?"

The football field was alive with pop music and hoards of people, many of them unfamiliar to Jenna. The Sports Boosters had commandeered the concession stand under the metal bleachers, and the mouthwatering aromas of hamburgers, French fries and chili dogs hung in the crisp afternoon air. Food and business booths spanned most of the end zone, but from the forty-yard line on, the field belonged to the noisily celebrating "flingers." Beau guided Jenna into a huge white tent where they registered and dropped off their fruitcakes and Food Bank donations—except for the two loaves in the plastic grocery bag slung over Jenna's arm.

Charity's volunteer firefighters were serving free hot beverages at one of the long tables. Beau dropped five dollars in the donation jar, then grabbed two hot ciders. "This is a quite a turnout. A lot bigger than I expected."

"Bigger than I expected, too," Jenna replied, accepting her cup and thanking him. "I just wish Aunt Molly were here. She would've loved this."

Beau tapped the cell phone case on his belt, visible beneath his leather jacket. "I'll take a few snapshots and send them to her phone when we get back to the Blackberry. But for now—" He grinned at the smiley-face stamp on the backs of their hands—their proof of registration. "Let's get in line and see what you're made of. I saw balloon launchers and catapults out there. The

Boy Scouts are going to have their hands full, cleaning up the mess."

Fish entered the tent as they prepared to leave. He raised a hand to stop their progress.

"Looks like we got a decent day for the fundraiser," he said when he reached them.

Beau answered. "Yep, no wind, temperature in the forties. Can't ask for more than that in mid-November in the Alleghenies."

"Well, we could," Fish replied, grinning. "It just wouldn't do much good."

Jenna spoke hesitantly. "But you didn't flag us down to discuss the weather."

Fish led them to a quiet corner. "We got the cell phone numbers from your phone company. Now we're waiting on a subpoena so the carrier will give up the identities of the subscribers. Looks like—"

"Identities?" Beau cut in. "Plural?"

Fish made a V of his fingers. "There were two different numbers. We tried them a bunch of times, but we never got an answer—just one of those 'This subscriber hasn't set up a voice mailbox yet' messages."

Jenna's voice trembled. "Does that mean they've been destroyed?"

"Can't tell. They could be turned off. But depending on what we find out, we might want to put a trace on your line. I'll let you know as soon as we hear anything."

Jenna nodded, but Beau sensed her anxiety building again.

"Anyway," Fish said, shifting his stance, then slowly moving away. "I gotta get back out there and relieve Charlie so he can grab something to eat. Man, I never thought this thing would bring in so many people."

When Fish was gone, Beau watched Jenna release a long, slow breath, then take a sip of her cider. He kept his voice low. "I know what you're thinking, and it's not necessarily true."

"It's Courtland. The subscriber names and addresses will be fake."

"Maybe. But try to stay positive."

"I am," she said. "I'm positive it's Courtland. And soon he'll get tired of this nasty little game of his and… and do something."

Beau felt a rush of frustration, but he kept his voice and expression as composed as he could. If Dane walked in right now, it would be his pleasure to rearrange the freak's aristocratic features. "Nothing's going to happen to you—not while I'm around."

"But you won't be around forever," she said, "and he's a very patient man. He's waited two years already, and according to information Detective Caspian gathered, he's relentless. He won't stop."

"Come on," Beau murmured, steering her deeper into the corner. All he wanted to do was hold her and tell her that he'd move Heaven and Earth to keep her safe. But he couldn't—not here. He settled for flipping up the puffy collar on her light blue quilted parka and resting his hands on her shoulders. "I'm not going anywhere," he said quietly. "You have my home and cell phone numbers. If you need me, I'll be there."

The fear in her eyes remained. "Why would you do that?"

"Because we're friends, and friends look out for each other. You have my word. If anyone scarier than the Easter Bunny approaches you, I'll make sure—"

"Hey, you two," a cheerful voice called behind them. "Is this a private party or can anyone join?"

Faintly annoyed by the interruption, but recognizing Rachel's voice, Beau glanced around and smiled. Jenna's anxious features cleared immediately, which didn't surprise him. She wasn't the type of woman who'd make her friends worry.

"Rachel, hi," she said. "Where's the new bridegroom today? Didn't he come with you?"

"He did, but the second we got here, Elmer Fox called Jake's cell to report shots fired on his land. Elmer thinks our local rednecks are rushing the deer season."

Jenna raised her eyebrows. "Elmer has Jake's cell phone number?"

Laughing, Rachel replied, "Oh, yeah. They're BFFs now—best friends forever." She raised the bag she carried. "That makes me the keeper of the fruitcakes until Jake gets back. He said he didn't expect to be gone long."

Beau spoke. "Well, until he shows up, why don't you hang out with us? We're just about ready to try our luck with the balloon launcher."

"Thank you very much," she said. "I accept."

The flinging didn't go well, but it was fun, and the shouting and laughter appeared to boost Jenna's morale. Or maybe Rachel's presence was the cause. Either way, after Jake found them, and they'd talked for a while, the four of them left the contest area and made their way to the concession stand. They were returning to the tent with their chili dogs and French fries when they passed Tammy Reston's pie booth. The tall man in the tailored black wool topcoat and white scarf who stood beside her appeared to be enjoying her company a little too much for a married man.

"Lawrence," Beau said, nodding.

Lawrence Chandler turned slightly to acknowledge

Beau's greeting, but his smile dissolved the instant he saw Jenna. The piercing look he sent her could've cut through steel. "Beau," he said with a curt nod. Then Chandler said something to Tammy, waved goodbye and left.

"Before you ask what that was all about," Jenna said. "I'm not one of his favorite people."

"So I gathered." Beau let her precede him into the noisy tent. "Is this about his son's trial?"

Jenna jerked a look back at him. "You know about that?"

"Aunt Molly told me."

"Of course she did," she said, sighing. Then she led them to a table in the rear of the tent that would accommodate the four of them, and the subject was shelved.

Beau couldn't wipe Chandler's look from his mind. An hour later, after speaking privately with Rachel and asking her to keep Jenna with her for a while, he told Jenna he needed to see a customer and would pick her up at the Campbells' when he was through. Her expression was easy to read. She was skeptical because they'd been together all day, and he hadn't mentioned it. Still, she didn't question him, and he was glad he didn't have to lie to her again.

The Chandlers lived two counties from Charity in a regal, two-story white brick home set on a hundred landscaped acres that shouted "money." A white brick four-stall garage sat back from the house, looking more like a second residence than a place to house vehicles. Lawrence Chandler's environmentally questionable Marcellus shale venture into gas and oil drilling had made him a millionaire many times over.

Beau parked his truck in the circular driveway

beside the stately entrance, then got out, ascended the steps and rang the bell. This was none of his business, but with all the weirdness going on in Jenna's life these past weeks, he had to ask a few questions.

Slender, attractive Devona Chandler came to the door moments after he rang the bell. Her blond-streaked dark brown hair was short and spiky, and huge gold hoop earrings scraped the shoulders of the silky green-and-gold paisley tunic she wore with solid green lounge pants.

"Beau," she said warmly. "How nice to see you again."

"You, too, Devona."

"Come in. What brings you way out here tonight?"

Beau stepped inside, took in the marble foyer, then brought his gaze back to Devona. "I need to talk to Lawrence. Is he around?"

Her warm tone cooled. "Unfortunately—or fortunately, depending on my mood—he's not here. He won't be back until I've moved out. Which, according to the letter I received from his attorney, had better be soon."

What did he say to that? "I'm sorry to hear that." Actually, he was sorry on two levels. He'd intended to ask Chandler point-blank if he'd been harassing Jenna. Chandler had undoubtedly handled thorny questions before, so questioning him wouldn't have bothered Beau in the least. Asking his wife the same thing wouldn't be that easy.

"It's for the best," she replied. "I'll be well compensated. He'd rather pay me off than face a judge whose ruling could cost him even more." She fiddled with the long gold chains she wore. "It's not as though we still love each other. Our son was the glue that held us together."

"I read about your son's conviction," Beau said kindly. "That had to be tough."

"More than you can imagine. His attorney is appealing again, but…" She let her statement trail, then went on. "Lawrence blamed me, of course. He said I coddled Timmy. But he was the one who bought him the fast car, and let him think he could do anything he pleased simply because he was a Chandler. The drinking, the girls… I hated it, but there was nothing I could do to stop the boys' club mentality that went on around here."

Beau saw the hurt in her eyes and wondered how much further he could go without causing more. The answer came quickly. He was here for Jenna. He'd go as far as he had to. "I need to ask you a hard question, Devona."

She hesitated for a few seconds, then said, "All right."

"My friend Jenna Harper was the jury foreperson on your son's case," he began.

She dropped her gaze. "I imagine she told you that I wasn't very nice to her."

"No, but I heard you were upset. What I need to know is, has there been any retaliation over your son's conviction?"

Devona looked honestly stunned. "Retaliation? No. No, of course not. Why? Has something happened?" Her tone took on a frightened note. "What has Lawrence done?"

"Maybe nothing. How did he take the verdict?"

"He came apart. He raged. He threatened. Timmy was his world."

Beau nodded, thinking that he might've come apart, too. "Do you know where he's staying now? I need to talk to him."

She shook her head. "We only communicate through our lawyers now, but I imagine he's still out of town on business. I'll let his attorney know that you'd like to speak with him."

"Thanks. Sorry to have bothered you." He handed her a business card with his home and cell phone numbers listed. As for Chandler's current lifestyle... It wasn't his place to tell Devona that a few hours ago, her husband had been less than sixty miles away.

"Don't apologize." She found a smile for him and opened the door. "It was a pleasure talking to a man who wasn't hurling insults. And Beau?"

"Yes?"

"I don't know what's going on with Ms. Harper, but I hope Lawrence isn't involved. He's a dirty fighter. Please tell her I regret what I said to her outside the courthouse."

Nodding grimly, then wishing her a good night, Beau got in his truck and headed for Jake Campbell's log home in the valley. He'd planned to keep quiet about his visit with Devona, thinking that his interference might make Jenna angry. Now he might have to reconsider.

ELEVEN

Sunday was warm by November's standards, and after church, Jenna and Beau joined the Campbells at the diner for brunch. Once or twice she'd scanned the crowd for that limping man in the tinted glasses, but for the most part, it was a fun outing that resulted in her falling even more deeply in love with Beau. Her day got even better when they returned to the Blackberry. When Beau mentioned moving the sitting room furniture to the dining room so he could start sanding, she'd used her employer clout to shut him down. "I have a better idea," she'd said. "This is the Lord's day. Let's make hot buttered popcorn and watch football instead."

It was the most wonderful day of her life—so wonderful, she had a hard time falling asleep that night. Jenna lay there in the dark, immersed in the heart-thrumming excitement that came with falling in love. For years, she'd chosen badly when it came to men, and she'd ended up being hurt when her trust was broken. That wouldn't happen this time. Beau was everything the others weren't. He was solid and dependable, sympathetic and caring without seeming weak. And it didn't hurt that those qualities came in a beautifully assembled, incredibly masculine package. "Please, Lord," she whispered. "Please let him love me, too."

She was still feeling that glow early Monday morning as she spread cherry filling between two of the chocolate layer cakes she'd baked last night. Then she added the last layer and frosted it with sweetened whipped cream before topping it with cherries and shaved chocolate. Rachel and Margo were coming by at one o'clock, and they loved Black Forest cake. She'd just popped it into the refrigerator when Beau came downstairs, said a pleasant "Good morning" and headed for the dining room.

Jenna followed. "You're not having breakfast?"

"Nope," he said. "I've put this off too long already."

"Can I help?"

"Not yet."

Jenna watched him move the dining room chairs to the back of the room, then slip plastic gliders under the table's legs and slide it easily across the hardwood to the wall where the chairs stood.

She held back a sigh. This wasn't the way she'd wanted their morning to begin. She didn't expect roses and love songs, but she'd hoped for conversation. More conversation than she'd had with Bernice before she'd rushed out again. "It was fun being with Rachel and Jake these past two days, wasn't it?"

"Yeah, it was," he said, distracted. He glanced around, seeming to measure the space they'd need for the sitting room's furniture. "Turns out Jake's a geocacher, too. We'll probably check out a few sites in the spring."

"I thought *we* were going in the spring."

He looked up suddenly as if surprised that she'd remembered—then the skin beside his dark eyes crinkled. "You and Rachel can go, too. If you want to, and she's up to it."

She wanted. Oh, yes, she wanted. On Saturday night when he'd come to pick her up at the Campbells', they'd stayed to talk over mugs of decaf and Rachel's oven-warm chocolate chip cookies. Conversation had flowed so easily, it was as though they'd been a foursome forever—which made Jenna see herself and Beau as a couple. That feeling had grown even stronger since their Sunday brunch and afternoon of popcorn and football.

"What's the smile about?" he asked as they passed through the French doors on their way to the sitting room.

"I don't know. I guess I'm just happy."

"Good," he said, smiling back. "Stay that way."

They'd just removed the dusty plastic sheets draped over the settees and started transferring furniture when the phone rang.

"Want me to get that?" he asked.

Jenna headed for the desk in the foyer. "No, I'll answer it." Nothing in the world could ruin this feeling of sublime satisfaction today. Not even a hang up. She checked the caller ID display, then answered on the third ring.

"Jenna, it's Fish. Is Beau there?"

"Yes, I'll get him for y—"

"No, don't do that," he said, something in his voice giving her pause. "I need to talk to you. Alone."

"Go on."

"The cell phone company we subpoenaed released the names of your hang-up callers." He hesitated. "Jenna, I'm sure there's an explanation for this because

I've known him for a long time, and I just don't see him doing anything like this."

Now she was really getting rattled. Someone Fish knew had made those calls? "Who? Who are you talking about?"

"Both cell phones are registered to Beau."

The news landed with a thud, but a split second later, Jenna shook off her doubts and fear stepped in. "It's not Beau. He wouldn't do that."

"I agree. But I'd like you to keep this to yourself for now. I'll be over to talk to both of you in a while. He'll have to supply an alibi for the date the phones were purchased in Ohio. I have to testify in a DUI case, first."

Then why call and tell her this ahead of time?

He seemed to read her mind. "I only called to give you a heads-up because when I saw the two of you at the fundraiser, it looked like you were sort of together. I wanted to give you time to think it through before you reacted."

"Thanks, but I wouldn't have needed time. I know who he is. See you in a while." She took a moment to consider what he'd said. Then suddenly she was angry and agitated and so afraid, she knew she'd never be able to hide it. She hurried into the hall. Regardless of Fish's request, Beau needed to know about this.

As she'd expected, the moment Beau saw her, he knew she was upset. He stopped in the middle of sliding the smaller of the two rose settees into the hall, a sheet of plastic trailing behind.

"What's wrong?"

"That was Fish on the phone."

The doorbell rang. Jenna froze, then looked nervously toward the front door. "I'll be right back." Then she strode back to the foyer and peered cautiously through the etched glass side light on the front door.

Holding a brown-paper wrapped package, Tammy Reston waited on the porch. Jenna's frazzled nerve endings curled into knots. She turned to Beau who'd followed her to the door.

His features darkened. "Are you expecting a delivery?"

She shook her head, then opened the door and Tammy stepped in from the cold. "Hi, Tammy."

"Hey, Jenna." She took in the man standing behind her. "'Mornin', Beau."

"Morning."

Tammy was a pretty blonde with the long, teased and sprayed hair of a country singer, and according to the bumper sticker on her truck, a proud member of the NRA. Out of necessity, her summer wardrobe—camouflage mini skirts and cropped tops—had been replaced by tight, white-gray-and-black camouflage pants tucked into high black boots and topped by a matching jacket cinched at the waist. Tammy ran Charity's sporting goods store, had a sideline parcel delivery business and sold blue-ribbon pies out of her back room. It was a mystery how she managed to hold down three jobs and still give the gossips something to talk about.

"Got a package for your aunt," she said, "but I hear she went to Connecticut for a few days."

Apparently, the local grapevine was still operating at top efficiency. "Yes, but she'll be back in a few days. Can I sign for the package?"

"Why yes, you can," she chirped, handing Jenna a pen and clipboard.

Jenna glanced at the glossy return address sticker on the box—and her tension eased. *Chang Chung's Gour-*

met Fortune Cookies. There was a colorful "Happy Birthday" sticker on the box as well. She sent up a silent prayer of thanksgiving. It was just a gift. Quickly signing, she exchanged the clipboard for the package and offered Tammy her thanks.

"No trouble," Tammy returned, waving off the tip Beau offered. "Just wish Ms. Jennings a happy birthday for me."

"I will," Jenna said. "Have a good day."

Tammy grinned and winked. "You two do the same." Then she hurried through the light flurries to her black truck.

Sighing, Jenna closed the door. "Well, it begins. Everyone she talks to today will know the innkeeper and the carpenter were all alone at the Blackberry before nine. Never mind that Bernice Gates was here until a few minutes ago."

"Thought you didn't care about gossip."

"I don't."

"Good," he said through a chuckle. "Because I hope she tells the whole town. Being with you can only elevate my bruised and battered reputation." He noted the return address on the package. "Fortune cookies?"

"Apparently," Jenna replied, eager to put the cookies aside and have that talk with him. "Looks like Millie took Aunt Molly at her word when she originally cancelled their plans. She had to have ordered these the second she hung up." She set the package on the desk. "I'll take these upstairs later. I need to talk to you about something."

He was already moving into the hall. "Okay, but let's talk while I finish moving that sofa into the dining room."

She was about to tell him what Fish said when she

noticed a small square of paper stuck to that trailing plastic sheet. She bent to pick it up. It wasn't square, it was oblong—one of Beau's business cards. She was in the process of handing it to him when she spotted her name written on the back—followed by a series of numbers.

Slowly, she brought the card close again and studied those numbers. Her heart nearly stopped beating. Jenna raised suddenly teary eyes to his. "What is this?"

Beau looked at her in surprise, then examined the card. "I don't know."

She couldn't recall ever feeling so sick. "Then let me tell you what it is. It's the number on the credit card I cancelled." Her tears were flowing freely now, and her heart was in shreds. He couldn't be responsible, yet those two cell phones had been registered to him, and he had her credit card number.

For several moments neither of them moved or spoke. Then, with a soft, "Thanks a lot," Beau turned and walked into the sitting room.

Jenna stood stone still while logic battled with her aching heart—and won. How could she have been so stupid? Beau had nothing to gain by involving himself in any of this. This was Courtland, pushing her buttons, trying to hurt her any way he could. She hurried after him. He'd gone back to the sitting room to work.

"Beau, I'm so sorry."

He didn't say a word, just continued slipping gliders under the second rose settee.

"Please listen. I told you a few minutes ago that it was Fish on the phone. He said they traced those cell phone numbers back to the source, and—and the source was you."

He jerked his head up from his task and his eyes went wide.

She rushed on. "I knew you weren't responsible for those hang-ups and that's exactly what I told Fish. But then I saw your business card and I put the two together, and just for a second—" She sent him a pleading look. "I'm so sorry."

"No problem," he said, continuing to work. "It's only natural that you'd come to that conclusion."

Natural because he'd grown up in squalor and some people had thought less of him because of it? The man who pretended he couldn't care less what people thought of him, cared a lot.

She touched his arm. "I made a mistake. I trust you. Now, please, let's talk about this. I don't know why Courtland would want to involve you in this, but the fact that he's aware that you're my…my friend…is frightening."

He ignored her last statement and centered on a previous one. "There's nothing to talk about. You trust me. We're fine." He slid the settee toward the doorway. "Now, I really need to get this into the other room."

Jenna's heart sank. "Let me help you."

"No, I'm okay. I'm not sure I can move the highboy alone, though, so I might need help then."

"Okay," she said quietly, knowing that they were far from fine. *Please, God,* she prayed silently. *Let him think this through and forgive me.* If he didn't she wouldn't be able to stand it.

He was sanding the floor and keeping to himself when Margo and Rachel arrived. Jenna walked them back to the sitting room so they could say hello, and he shut off the sander. But his smile and easy conversation were for them, not her, and it hurt. Saying he'd finish later so they didn't have to shout over the noise, he washed up, grabbed his jacket and headed for the door.

Jenna followed.

"I'll be back later," he said.

"Where are you going?"

"I need to see Fish about this cell phone business. After that, I'll probably pick up something at the diner and check my house. Please call my cell phone—my *only* cell phone—before your friends leave, and I'll come back. Aunt Molly doesn't want you to be alone."

Jenna swallowed the emotional lump in her throat, then watched him back his truck out of his space and drive off. The message was clear. If he hadn't promised Aunt Molly to stick around, he'd be history now. Rachel and Margo were sitting on the turquoise sofa and talking quietly when she entered the parlor.

Never one to mince words, Margo spoke. "Okay, what's going on? When I picked up Rachel, she said you and Beau were getting close. That didn't look like 'close' to us."

Jenna sat in the wing chair across from them. When Margo was Charity's chief of police, she'd worn her dark hair pulled back in a bun. Today, it fell in loose, brown waves to her shoulders. She looked trim and pretty in jeans, sneakers and a black jewel neck sweater. "Did Rachel fill you in on what's been happening here for the past two weeks?"

Margo darted a look at Rachel, and Rachel answered. "No, I thought it would be better coming from you."

She was right. Then Margo would only have to hear the information once. "Let's talk in the kitchen."

When the coffee was poured and the cake served,

Jenna sat. She started with the identity theft and funeral flowers, then continued through the ant problem, razors in the mattress and hang-ups. Finally, she told Margo about the cell phones and planted business card.

"I handled it so badly," she said, tearing up and suddenly unable to sit any longer. She took the carafe to the coffeemaker and topped it off, then returned it to the table. "I thought of the time he'd spent here, everything he had access to…coming and going as he pleased… And for a few seconds, I was afraid he might be involved." She swallowed. "It only took me a minute to realize that he had nothing to gain by it, and I apologized. But I was a minute too late. The damage was done."

Margo rose and gave her a hug. "He's a smart man. He'll forgive you."

"Will he? One summer while I was visiting my aunt and Beau was doing her yard work, he told me something. I can't remember what led to it, but he said he'd been shunned so many times he was beginning to think he was Amish. He laughed, but I know it bothered him. Now I'm afraid he thinks… Well, you know."

Margo frowned. "I'm glad Aunt Molly's out of town. This is no place for her right now. How are *you* doing—other than this thing with Beau?"

"About as well as you'd expect. I'm almost certain Courtland's behind every nasty thing that's been done, but I desperately want to believe it's someone else." She shook her head. "And speaking of Aunt Molly, I need to phone her. She'll want to thank Millie for the gift that came this morning."

"Millie sent Aunt Molly a package when she knew she'd be seeing her?"

"I assume so since it came from their favorite Chinese restaurant. Aunt Molly loves their fortune cookies. Millie must've mailed them as soon as Aunt Molly bailed out on the trip."

"She bailed, then changed her mind?"

"Yes, after Beau promised to stay until she came back."

"Show me the package."

A few minutes later, the three of them were standing in the foyer, and Jenna's heart was beating double-time. Gripping the phone's handset in a stranglehold, she continued to speak to her aunt. "Millie didn't send the cookies?"

"No. I'm coming home, Jenny."

"Don't do that. I'm okay. Maybe this is just a coincidence. You probably mentioned liking the cookies to one of your other friends. After our lunch at the diner, half the town knows about your birthday."

"Maybe." She drew a breath. "Is Beau there?"

No, and she wished so much that he was. "He had to run an errand, but Margo and Rachel are here."

"Then open the box. See if there's a card inside."

Gooseflesh covered her arms as Jenna stared at the parcel. It wasn't heavy enough to be a bomb—although she was hardly an authority on explosives. How much did bombs weigh? And did they actually tick? Also the box had been postmarked in Ohio, and the return address sticker looked authentic.

She met Margo's eyes. "She wants us to open the box."

"Tell her you'll call her back in a few minutes. I don't want to sound like a conspiracy theorist, but I think we should open it outside."

When she'd done as Margo asked, they stepped out on the back porch and set the box on the wide railing.

There was no card or message inside. There was nothing in the box but a dozen chocolate and vanilla-iced fortune cookies decorated with colorful candy sprinkles.

"There's a phone number on the address sticker," Jenna said, picking up the box and moving back into the kitchen. "I'll call and see who ordered them."

Rachel spoke up. "I think you should open one of them first. Maybe the cookies are personalized, and the sender's name is inside."

That wasn't a bad idea. Reopening the box, Jenna chose a chocolate iced cookie. "I'll just wiggle one of the fortunes out. This one looks fairly loose." The bottom fell out of her stomach when she read it, then handed it to Rachel.

Soon, the three of them were staring at twelve identical slips of paper. Every one of them said, "Life is short. Enjoy it while you can."

Jenna ripped off the return address label and went to the phone. A woman with a heavy Chinese accent said, "Chang Chung's Gourmet Cookies. How may I help you?"

Jenna drew a shaky breath. "You can tell me who sent a box of your fortune cookies to my home."

Beau pulled into the driveway, parked to the left of the inn, then shut off his engine and sank back against the seat. Okay, he was being too thin-skinned and he knew it. But he couldn't get past that look of betrayal in her eyes. It made no difference that she'd done a quick about-face; for a full minute, she'd actually thought he was capable of the lousy, underhanded things that had been done to her. Nothing had hurt that badly in a long, long time.

As a kid, he'd mostly walked away from the bad stuff. When Jasper had pushed him around and called him worthless, he'd simply taken off—which was pretty much what his grandfather had wanted anyway. And he'd tried to see the good inside him that he knew was there but seemed invisible to some people around him.

That wasn't an option now. He'd made Aunt Molly a promise and he'd take another emotional beating before he let her down. Besides, he had too much pride to leave his work for someone else to complete.

He got out of the car, walked to the front door and rang the bell. There was no way he'd use the security code. Not because he was "in a cowardly little snit" as Jasper used to say, but because some sappy part of him wouldn't give her any more reason to worry. She worried enough.

Throwing open the door, Margo breezed past him, pulling on her jacket. Beau's protective instincts flared again.

"Margo?"

She motioned behind her as she continued to stride toward her vehicle. Jenna and Rachel stood in the foyer. "Jen will tell you. I'll be back soon. I need to grab something from my house."

With a questioning look for Jenna, he stepped inside. Instead of answering, she said quietly, "I'm glad you're back."

"I'll let you two talk," Rachel said, then politely disappeared.

Beau met the turmoil in Jenna's eyes. Regardless of her soft tone, he could see that she was barely keeping it together. "What happened?"

"Not here," she murmured.

To his confusion, she opened the door, walked coatless to his truck and climbed inside. A moment later, he was settled behind the wheel and turning on the heater. "Where are we going?"

"Nowhere. I just didn't want to talk in there." She folded her hands on her lap and drew a shaky breath. "The fortune cookies weren't for Aunt Molly. They were for me. He knew I'd refuse an unexpected package."

Beau's heartbeat quickened. "How do you know that?"

"Because Millie didn't send them. Aunt Molly asked me to open the box to see if there was a card inside. There was no card—only twelve cookies with identical personalized messages. They all said, 'Life is short. Enjoy it while you can.' No friend would send an eighty-five-year-old woman a gift like that."

It was hard to control his anger. When was this going to end? "Why didn't you call the police? I just came from there, and no one mentioned—"

"I'll call when Margo gets back. Unless he sees more evidence, Perris will insist that there's nothing threatening about those 'fortunes,' and remind me that the package was sent to my aunt, not me."

"What evidence?"

She sent him a weary look. "He had to have learned about Aunt Molly's trip days ago to have the personalized cookies sent in time for her birthday. As far as I know, we're the only people who discussed it." She nodded toward the Blackberry's pretty front door. "In there."

The reason for Margo's swift departure quickly dawned. "She's bringing back a bug detector, isn't she?"

"Yes. She said a man with money can pay for a lot more than ants and razor blades. She's going to sweep for wireless cameras and listening devices. If she finds anything, Perris will have to take this seriously."

Now he wasn't sure what to hope for—bugs or no bugs. "If your Mrs. Bolton planted bugs, whoever's behind this knows about more than your aunt's love of fortune cookies."

Jenna whirled on him. "Why do you keep saying *whoever's* behind this? I've told you repeatedly that the man who tried to kill me—the man who left me for dead—the man who might've taken away any chance I have of conceiving a child of my own, has a name. *Courtland Dane.*"

Beau went deathly still, stunned by her anger, and even more stunned by her words. The sympathy in his eyes seemed to deflate her, and she looked away. Obviously, she hadn't meant to share as much as she had. He waited another moment before he spoke. "I'm sorry."

She continued to stare through the side window at the rhododendron bushes fronting the porch. "There are worse things."

Yes, there were. At least she was alive. But he wouldn't offer platitudes—even deeply felt platitudes—because anything he said might seem to trivialize her loss, and there was nothing trivial about it. He *could* offer support. "You said he *might've* taken away any chance of you're having a child. That sounds encouraging."

"My doctor said it's still possible."

"Then we'll both pray that it happens. Do you want to go back inside now?"

She gave him a sad look. "No, if it's okay with you, I'd rather sit out here and wait for Margo. I feel hunted in there. She shouldn't be long."

"Whatever you want. While we wait, can I tell you

something that might make a difference in the way you see things? I don't want to upset you any more than you are."

"I don't see how you could."

"Okay, then." He drew a breath. It was time to tell her about his visit with Devona Chandler.

She listened quietly, without stopping him, but he could tell that she didn't have much faith in the possibility that Chandler was her tormentor. She was tied too tightly to the past and the monster who'd cut her.

He'd finished, and she was thanking him for going out of his way to help her when Margo's gold SUV sped up the driveway and swerved into a parking space on the right. They were both out of the truck in an instant.

Jenna reached Margo before he did. "Success?" she asked nervously.

Margo flashed a device about the size of a cell phone. "I thought Cole might've had both of them in Florida, but there was one at the house. Come on. Let's see what this thing can do."

Twenty minutes later, with a music station blaring in the kitchen and forecasters on the parlor's TV set predicting heavy snow for the northeast, the four of them talked in Jenna's quarters. Beau took the wing chair, while Margo and Rachel pressed close to Jenna on the sofa. They'd all agreed that since Mrs. Bolton had to have planted the bugs after lights-out, that Margo's and Aunt Molly's rooms were "clean." They were right. Other rooms weren't as pristine.

Margo's sweep of the inn had turned up five bugs. One behind a switch plate, one in the suspended light above the kitchen's work island, one inside a lamp in the Blue Room, and one inside the highboy that had been transferred to the dining room.

"I don't understand," Jenna said, staring morosely at the last one, a disabled "pen" bug Margo had discovered among those crammed into a mug on the desk. "Don't these things have to be retrieved to get information?"

Margo set the now-inoperable pen on the coffee table. "Not this type—and they don't record, they transmit and they're easy to get. Almost any store that specializes in electronics handles surveillance equipment. They might not advertise or feature them in their store windows, but if a troubled parent wants to know if her babysitter is letting her toddler cry too long... Well, wireless bugs and 'nanny-cams' are very available, and they're not expensive. If Mom strikes out at the electronics store, there's always the internet."

Beau watched Rachel squeeze Jenna's hand, and he expelled a sigh. His head was so messed up where she was concerned, he didn't know up from down anymore. "How far do these things transmit?"

"That depends on the type of bug. They transmit on an FM signal, so someone could listen in just by tuning in on an FM radio while they're parked across the street. Other wireless bugs send a signal to a receiver where conversations can be recorded. Some can send out a signal three to five miles away."

Jenna's voice shook. "What about the bugs you found here? What kind are they? How—how far away is he?"

Margo spoke gently. "I'm sorry. I can't be sure because this really isn't my area of expertise. All I know for sure is, you need to decide if you want to leave the bugs in place and feed this jerk false information—or get rid of them."

"I want them gone."

"Okay," Margo said. "Let's call Perris. He'll probably want to remove them himself, then check the bugs and the area around them for prints. Hopefully, they'll have serial numbers on them that can be traced back to the person who bought them."

She smiled a little. "I'd suggest that you get out of town for a while, but if you *are* in danger, and this isn't someone's idea of a sick joke, you're probably safer here than anywhere else."

Beau watched thoughts cloud Jenna's eyes while she seemed to work through a problem. Then she drew a breath, looked at him and raised her chin. "Do you remember what you said the other day about missing out on what life has to offer?" He nodded slowly, half afraid of what she would say next. Then she said it. "I have a self-defense class tonight."

Rachel touched her arm. "Jen, I don't think that's a good idea. You've talked about the classes openly. The person who's listening knows your schedule."

"I know, and I thank you for caring," Jenna replied. "But he also knew my schedule on Thursday and Friday, and he knew Beau and I would be taking Aunt Molly to the airport. Nothing happened. I think he's waiting until he can get me alone—the way it was the first time."

Beau spoke up. "Jenna, listen to your friends."

"You made me a promise," she said, her attention fully on him again. "You said you'd take me to class and drive me home. You said nothing would happen to me while you were around. Well? Are you going to be around?"

TWELVE

Jenna sat silently before Chief Lon Perris's desk, flanked by Margo and Beau. Behind them, a low spindled gate divided the reception area and Sarah French's empty desk from the wood-paneled office proper. Perris's black mood hadn't improved since Margo had pointed out the electronic bugs. She'd aggravated him even more by respectfully suggesting that Jenna work with an officer on the department's facial composite software. Since the description of "Mrs. Bolton" hadn't produced any leads, she'd thought a computer sketch might be helpful. At the very least, it couldn't hurt.

Perris had gone beet-red. Clearly, he didn't like being upstaged, particularly by a female predecessor who knew which tools he had at his disposal. Now, dropping into his chair and tipping back, he addressed Jenna.

"As Ms. Blackburn might've mentioned, our facial composite program isn't as effective as an artist's rendering or the expensive whole-face software many big city departments are using. That's the reason I didn't suggest this in the first place. However," he said after clearing his throat, "since you want to try it, Officer Troutman is setting up in the interrogation room. In a few minutes, I'll escort you back there where you'll be asked to choose rather basic individual facial features from a database in order to create a likeness of your guest."

He thought this was a waste of time, Jenna decided, but she was willing to try anything to stop this nightmare. She'd hoped to learn something from the woman at Chang Chung's, but there was no help there. The man who'd ordered and paid cash for the personalized cookies was short and thin with average looks. There was nothing distinctive about him.

Perris was still speaking. "Take your time. I'm sure your friends can find something to do until you're finished."

Beau spoke. "If it's all the same to you, I wouldn't mind sitting in on the process."

"Neither would I," Margo said.

Perris sent her a smile that put her in her place. "I'm sorry, but having her posse in the room might be distracting for Ms. Harper. You're welcome to help yourselves to coffee or a soft drink from the machine while you wait." He nodded to a row of chairs near the door. "Out there."

Beau sent Perris a slow smile. "Maybe we'll just head across the street to the diner until Jenna's finished." He reached out as if to touch her shoulder, then to Jenna's disappointment, withdrew his hand before he made contact. "Call my cell when you're finished, okay?"

"I will. Thank you."

Then Margo wished her luck, and with a heavy heart, Jenna watched them leave. Beau's feelings for her had cooled. But at least he wasn't treating her as badly as she'd treated him.

* * *

Two hours later, dressed in light blue sweats with her hair tied back, Jenna entered the community center and walked with Beau to the meeting room where her class was about to begin. He laid her jacket on one of the chairs against the wall, then faced her soberly. "I'll see you in a little while. Have a good lesson."

"I'll try," she replied.

She was trying to stay joyful, but with conversation between them so polite now, it took a lot of work. When she'd finished at the police station and they'd all returned to the Blackberry, Beau had immediately plugged the sander back in and gone to work. It was as if he couldn't finish quickly enough and get out of her life. Seeing her disappointment, Margo had gently reminded her that hers and Cole's path to the altar hadn't been easy, either, but they'd come through the tough times stronger than ever because they'd loved each other.

"But Beau doesn't love me," she'd said.

"Because he hasn't said it?" Margo asked, then smiled. "I see the way he looks at you. This bodyguard business isn't totally about Aunt Molly's wishes. He cares. Give him time."

Her class was energizing and confidence-building, and when it ended, Jenna had the sense that she *would* be able to fight back if the need arose again. In fact, by the time Beau returned to pick her up, she was determined to fight back emotionally, too, and with help from God, regain the ground she'd lost with him.

He was seated in a dimly lit Italian restaurant enjoying a dinner of veal parmigiana with Portobello mushrooms when the cell phone in his suit jacket's inside pocket vibrated. Daubing the corners of his mouth with his napkin, then smoothing his mustache, he retrieved it and lifted it to his ear.

He spoke over the instrumental music—*Torna a Surriento.* "Yes?"

"Trouble."

His tranquil mood vanished. If there was one word he did not want to hear from his associates, it was *trouble.* He sat back, half-hidden behind a wooden lattice panel laced with grapevines. "What kind of trouble?"

"They found the bugs. An ex-cop friend of hers wondered how the anonymous gift-giver knew about the old lady's penchant for fortune cookies and decided the place was wired."

Anger cinched his throat and he felt his face redden. He'd lost his pipeline—*his deeply satisfying pipeline*—to her fear and misery. "What was said before you lost the connection?"

"We think the carpenter's history. Or soon will be. Right after she learned that the old cells were registered to Travis, she found the business card."

"She blames him?"

"She did at first, then did an about-face. But by the time she apologized, he'd had it with her. I don't think he'll stick around long."

At least that was gratifying. Travis's alibi regarding the cell phones would hold up. But together, those phones and business card had driven a wedge between them, so they'd served their purpose. Sadly, Jenna had cancelled her credit card before the power tools Deirdre ordered could be delivered to Travis. That would've assured the carpenter's departure from her life.

"Now what?"

He thought for a moment. "Keep an eye on their comings and goings. Use both vehicles."

"Way ahead of you. Gotta go. They're just leaving the community center. I'm parked—get this—across the street from the police station."

"Don't be smug. Be careful. Have you purchased the device and arranged for the rental?"

"We're ready to go, and the rental is in place. Are you?"

"Yes. I'm ready."

Jenna stirred in her sleep, burrowing deeper into the covers, frowning as she dreamed. Beau was barefooted in the snow, swinging an axe, chopping firewood to keep them warm. But somehow, the deep cuts in the log filled in again, and he had to start over. And she was so cold.

Slowly coming awake, she opened her eyes in the darkness, then realized that her absurd dream was centered in reality. The temperature in her bedroom had dropped. As usual, she'd lowered the thermostat serving the first floor before bedtime, but apparently, she'd taken it too low. She glanced at the clock on her nightstand. It wasn't quite two.

Slipping into her robe, she padded barefoot through the hall, then went into the parlor where a Tiffany lamp burned just brightly enough for navigation. Briefly, she nudged the thermostat up a little, then headed back to bed. She was slipping under the covers when she heard the solid thud of a car door closing.

Every hair on her head prickled.

Bolting out of bed again, she hurried across the hall to the window in the empty sitting room, only half aware of the sandy grit under her feet. She peeked through the ornamental mesh—searched the area near the three stall garage to her right. Nothing moved. Nothing but the softly falling snow.

A floorboard creaked behind her, and Jenna spun around.

"It's just me," Beau said quietly. "I heard it, too. Don't worry. No one can get in without tripping the alarm, and that should discourage anybody." He'd pulled on jeans and a dark sweatshirt, but he was bare-foot, too. Picking up a length of baseboard, he continued to keep his voice low. "Stay here. I think I heard a car leave, but I want to look around."

"I'm going with you."

"Jenna, please."

"No."

They moved into the hall, passing her quarters and approaching the parlor. He reached around the corner and felt for the dimmer switch—turned off the lamp. Then they were in the foyer where the lighting was also muted.

"Call the station," Beau murmured. But Jenna was already slipping behind the desk and reaching for the phone. Maybe it was nothing, she thought, praying it was true. Just a traveler who'd lost his way and turned around in the driveway. If it was nothing, Perris or whoever answered the call would just have to understand.

But why would a traveler open and shut his car door? To check his position? Was the snow that deep? Jenna picked up the handset.

Her heart shot into her throat when the front door opened, and a small, dark figure moved inside.

"Stop right there!" Beau shouted. He hit the light switch, flooding the foyer with two hundred-fifty watts of startling chandelier light.

Aunt Molly's blue eyes went wide with horror.

For a long second none of them moved. Then, releasing a ragged breath, Beau lowered his weapon, leaned the baseboard against the desktop and pinned a disbelieving look on their pint-sized intruder.

Jenna rushed around the desk to her. "Aunt Molly, what are you doing here?"

"I live here," she said, fully recovered now and removing her black pillbox hat. She handed it to Jenna, then loosened the frog fasteners on her matching coat. "I couldn't stay away when I might be needed here."

Beau still looked stunned. "Where's your luggage?"

"The airline lost it. They say it'll be here tomorrow." She nodded at the keypad behind the desk. "Now somebody better push some buttons and reset the security system, or it's going to get noisy around here."

A creaking noise came from the staircase above, spinning the three of them around. Wrapped in a canary-yellow pile robe, Bernice Gates peered down at them from the railing, curlers in her tinted red hair and a shocked expression on her face. "Jenna?" she asked timidly. "Is everything all right?"

Fifteen minutes later, after assurances and introductions had been made and Bernice had returned to her room, Molly sat beside Jenna on the parlor's sofa. As she sipped decaffeinated tea, she explained her unexpected arrival. "After I called back and you told me about the cookies, I was so upset, I booked a flight to Pittsburgh. I took a taxi from there."

Beau sighed. "You should've called me. I could've saved you a bundle."

"Thank you, but you had other things to do, and the money meant nothing to me."

That was certainly true, Jenna thought. Her aunt

often said that the only thing money was good for was helping others and buying the things we needed. Other than that, it was only so much paper and tin.

"My driver was a lovely young Asian woman who kept me entertained the entire way home with stories about her life in Taiwan. It was quite enjoyable." The lines in her face deepened then. "With the snow coming, I was afraid that if I didn't leave immediately, I might not get home for Thanksgiving." She set her tea cup aside. "Now tell me what Chief Baboon had to say about that gift box so we can all get some sleep."

She wasn't pleased with the report, but she was glad Jenna used the department's facial composition program—even though it didn't turn out that well.

"What about contacting the cookie company?" Molly asked. "Did anyone do that?"

"I did," Jenna said. "Then Perris tried his luck, but the man who sent them paid cash, and no one there could give us a description." She lowered her voice. "I wish you'd stayed in Connecticut."

Molly rose. "I'm exactly where I want to be. And now it's time I toddled up to my room. It's nearly three o'clock, and I need my beauty sleep."

Jenna bent to hug her. "Night, Aunt Molly."

"Good night, dear. I'll see you when the sun makes an appearance." She patted Beau's arm. "You get some sleep, too."

"I'm on my way right now. I'll follow you upstairs."

Molly started into the foyer, then suddenly turned to glance between the two of them. "On second thought," she said, "why don't you go on ahead? I just remembered something I have to discuss with Jenna." She wrinkled her nose. "Girl stuff."

Beau paused for a moment, silently doubting her excuse. Then he said good-night and climbed the stairs.

Molly didn't speak until they heard his footfalls on the floor above them. "What happened?"

"What happened?" Jenna repeated.

"Between you and Beau. When I left, the two of you were smiling at each other like lovebirds. Now you barely make eye contact."

Jenna glanced away, feeling the sting of tears in her eyes. "It's a long story."

Molly led her back to the sofa. "I have all night."

"You need to sleep."

"I'll sleep when I'm dead. Tell me what happened."

The aroma of coffee brewing woke Jenna the next morning. Glancing at her clock and seeing that it was already eight-thirty, Jenna showered and dressed quickly in jeans and a rose-colored sweatshirt, then made her way to the kitchen. Beau stood beside the coffeemaker, waiting for the carafe to fill. Beyond the kitchen window, it was snowing again.

"Good morning," she said, trying on a smile. "Thanks for starting the coffee."

"You're welcome. What time did you two finally get to bed?"

"I'm not sure," she said, wishing he'd smiled back. She took two heavy white mugs and the sugar bowl from an upper cupboard. "Four o'clock? A little after?" She retrieved a container of half-and-half from the refrigerator and set it on the counter. He looked good in a hunter-green short-sleeved knit pullover and jeans—far better than he should have after being up during the night. "Did you sleep well?"

"Better—or at least longer—than you did."

"I know. I'll be a zombie by midday."

He watched coffee drip into the carafe for a few moments, then glanced briefly at her. "I vacuumed the sitting room while you were asleep, so in a few minutes, I'll wipe the floor down with a damp rag. Unfortunately, it has to be cleaned with mineral spirits, too, and I'm hesitant to do that with Aunt Molly and Mrs. Gates here."

Jenna took her time taking a spoon from the silverware drawer. "Bernice is undoubtedly gone for the day, but we can ask Aunt Molly what she wants to do when she gets up."

The coffeemaker began to spit and gurgle. Shutting it off, Beau filled their mugs, then watched while she stirred sugar and creamer into hers. When she looked up, his gaze had softened slightly, and Jenna felt her heart quicken. Maybe he was coming around. *Please, God.*

"So other than not getting much sleep, how are you doing?"

She shrugged. "Nothing's changed. I'm still afraid, and I'm trying not to be. Sometimes I think I'm successful. Sometimes I know I'm not."

His grim expression told her he'd recognized that. "I find myself thinking about all the things that have happened."

"Me, too."

"Yeah, I know. But my thoughts are probably different from yours. I've been thinking that this sort of thing could go on forever without any real harm coming to you. If Dane's the guy doing this—and I know I'm pushing my luck, using the *if* word—it was pretty gutsy of him to cut you and risk everything he'd worked for. So why, now that he's a wanted man, would he hire people to mess with you—not get rid of you? If this Mrs. Bolton could plant bugs, razor blades and one of my business cards—and access your password-protected computer—what would've prevented her from picking the lock on your room and quietly killing you in your sleep?

Jenna felt herself pale. "What a lovely thought."

He softened his tone. "You know what I mean. If he wanted revenge, that would've been more straightforward."

The phone rang, and Jenna froze, wondering absurdly if discussing Courtland had conjured him up.

"I'll get it," Beau said, already moving. "It's probably someone wanting to book a room."

"Thanks," she returned, knowing that should've been her first thought. Not every phone call was related to her fear.

This one was.

Beau gave her the handset. "It's Detective Caspian from the Detroit PD."

Jenna took the phone quickly. "Detective? Is there news?"

"Good morning, Ms. Harper. Nothing definite, but after we spoke a while ago, I had some time, so I did some more digging. I can't tell you where he is now, but four months ago, an acquaintance of his spotted someone who looked like Dane in Barbados."

"Four months ago?" she repeated. "But you said none of his associates had—"

"I know. This guy was never questioned because we didn't know about him. He did relay the information to our department, but…I'm sorry…there was a mix-up and it never got to me."

Jenna felt a tiny ray of hope. "Did he speak to Courtland?"

"No. I just got off the phone with him. He said that he called to him, but when the man spotted him, he dissolved into a crowd of tourists."

"But he's sure it was Courtland?"

"Not a hundred percent, but he feels confident that it was." He drew a breath. "Now, I know it's not what you hoped to hear. But if he was in Barbados in June or July, he could still be there."

"Or not."

"Yes. But he's a wanted man, and airport security is tighter than ever now."

Did that also apply to ships? There was a lot of water between the lower Antilles and the United States, but that was small comfort. Somehow she didn't see the same airport-security vigilance being attached to tourists on vacation. She saw Beau's questioning look, then shook her head to tell him it wasn't bad news.

"That's about all I have for you now," Caspian went on. "I just wanted you to know there's a chance he's not even in the country. I hope that makes you feel a little better."

Jenna hooked a lock of hair behind her ear. "To be honest, I'm not sure how I feel. But thank you for calling—and caring."

"Glad to do it. Bye, now."

"Goodbye, and thanks again."

Jenna replaced the handset, then walked back to where Beau still stood beside the coffeemaker. She answered the query in his eyes. "There's a chance Courtland's been living in Barbados. An acquaintance believes he saw him there this past summer."

"That's good—with respect to what's happening to you."

"Yes, it is," she said, feeling her stomach quake. "If he's still there."

THIRTEEN

The wind blew, light snow flying by the window as the weatherman on the kitchen's small TV tracked the northeast's first big snowstorm of the season. Aunt Molly had made an appearance around nine-twenty, dressed in a long navy velveteen skirt, and a pink-and-navy paisley blouse, but Jenna doubted she'd be in them for long. Losing sleep had taken the bounce out of her step. She'd be napping soon. Her flagging energy aside, however, she'd been overjoyed to learn about Jenna's conversation with Detective Caspian.

She took a warm croissant from the basket Jenna placed on the table, then spread it with butter and orange marmalade. "Have they notified the Barbados authorities?"

"I'm not sure. Caspian didn't say." The low growl of the snow blower carried to them from outside as Beau continued to clear a driveway that didn't need clearing yet. But he'd wanted something to do, probably because there *was* nothing for him to do, and the distance and tension between them was making them both uncomfortable.

"Well, call me vengeful, but I want to see that horrid man extradited and sent back here to stand trial."

At Any Cost

"Likewise," Jenna replied, filling their teacups. She dredged up a smile she didn't feel, and changed the subject. "Reverend Landers's wife phoned a little while ago with a reminder to be at the fellowship hall by 10:00 a.m. on Wednesday to start preparing the turkeys. She was glad to hear you'd come back early."

"Oh? Is she short of help?"

"Actually, no. Counting Bernice and the others who've come in for their anniversary, she has sixteen volunteers to serve and bus tables, and quite a few of them are also donating pies. I offered to bring a few, too, but she said we didn't have to since we're making the dressing."

They were discussing her visit with Millie when the kitchen door opened, and Beau stepped inside. Careful of the snow on his boots, he stayed on the mat. His smile was for Aunt Molly.

"Hey," he teased. "You're up."

"I am, indeed. Did you miss me?"

"Absolutely. And now I'm leaving."

Molly chuckled. "You must've missed me a lot. Where are you going?"

"The new building supply house out near the mall." He pulled off his gloves and stuffed them in the pockets of his leather jacket. "I've been hesitant to clean the sitting room floor because the fumes from mineral spirits can be nasty. In fact, Jenna and I talked about moving you and Mrs. Gates elsewhere to avoid the fumes."

Clapping her hands together, Molly exclaimed, "What a lovely phrase!"

Beau frowned curiously. "What phrase?"

"*Jenna and I.* But go on."

His rugged features clouded, and feeling horribly uneasy, Jenna busied herself buttering a croissant she didn't want. She loved her aunt's unbridled honesty, but she really wished she'd bridle it when Beau was in the room.

"Anyway," he said, ignoring Molly's words, "I did some phoning this morning, and E-Z Builders has a citrus-based solvent that will be a lot easier on our respiratory systems. I'm going out there to pick some up."

"I'll get my wallet," Jenna said.

He finally spoke to her. "No, I have an account there. We can settle up later."

Of course he had an account there, Jenna thought, embarrassed. He was a contractor, not a friend who was doing her a favor. He'd just add the cost to the bill. "Be careful on the roads."

"The highway crews have been around, and the snow's only deep where it's drifted. I should be back in an hour or so. I want to stop at my shop afterward and grab a set of kneepads."

He opened the kitchen door, then stepped out on the enclosed back porch. Wind whistled around the corner of the inn. "Don't forget to lock up behind me."

"I won't. See you soon."

"And on that happy note," Aunt Molly said, "I shall finish my croissant and carry my tea back up to my rooms."

Jenna stared at her, startled. "Why? You just came downstairs."

"Because I'm tired, and when he gets back the two of you need to talk through this thing or there'll be no fixing it."

Tears stung Jenna's eyes. "I tried. When I apologized, he said things between us were fine, but as you can see, they're not. It'll take a miracle for him to forgive me."

"Then talk to the Man in charge of miracles." She scanned Jenna's clothing. "However, since the Lord helps those who help themselves, it wouldn't hurt for you to look irresistible when Beau comes back. We Harper women have always dressed for our men. You look lovely in your sweatshirt, dear, but unfortunately, the message it sends is take me to a sporting event. Not meet me at the altar."

His cell phone vibrated as he brushed snow from the windshield of his slowly heating rental car. Eager for an update, he pulled it from the inside pocket of his dark topcoat.

"Yes?"

"How close are you?"

He recognized Thug Number Two's voice—the short, skinny one. "Forty-five minutes."

"The carpenter's gone, and she's alone."

A rush of anticipation heated his blood. "Make sure the sled can't be seen from the road. I don't want some idiot stealing it before it serves its purpose." Ending the call, he slid inside the Chrysler and double-checked the instrument panel's GPS against the page he'd downloaded from the internet. Both waypoints—the "parking" and "destination" coordinates—were correct. He then took a handheld GPS from his pocket and did the same, though there was only one waypoint on the display.

He knew he probably wouldn't need the portable unit. The snowmobile's tracks would be easy to follow. But he wasn't leaving anything to chance. He turned on the defroster, waited for the windshield to clear, then headed for the small restaurant down the road to have a leisurely breakfast before he went to work.

The storm that had been forecasted was well on its way. He couldn't have chosen a better day.

Beau drove through the blowing snow, his wipers keeping time with the Eddie Rabbit tune on the radio. He had a new "ear worm." Usually it was a song that wouldn't go away. Today it was the constant repetition of Aunt Molly's less than subtle words. During the past week, he'd come very close to thinking in "Jenna and I" terms. But having her doubt his integrity had taken a sledge hammer to any thoughts he'd had about a future with her. He couldn't be with a woman who didn't trust him.

He cruised down Main Street where two firemen in cherry pickers fought the wind while trying to string lights and garlands high over the street. He beeped and waved, and Joe Reston and Ray Blair waved back. Across the street at the bakery, one of the cashiers was hanging a huge wreath in the long, wide plate glass window. And suddenly all that pre-Christmas joy made him feel lonely.

He reached the outskirts, passing the strip mall and watching through the intermittent slap of his wipers for E-Z Builder's long red roof. It came into view. Fifteen minutes later, the solvent was on the floor in his backseat, and he was heading for the kneepads in his shop. The sooner he finished the floor, the sooner he could complete his work and get back to the life he'd had before he started this job. He just couldn't handle being around her anymore.

His cell phone chimed. Keeping his eyes on the road, he took it from his belt and said hello. The male caller's voice was low and angry with a dash of malice. "I got your message," Lawrence Chandler said without pre-

amble. "Now I have one for you. Stay away from my
wife and out of my business. If anything the two of you
discussed becomes an embarrassment to me, I will ruin
you." Then he hung up before Beau could respond.

Beau pulled off the side of the road and hit a number
on his speed dial.

Putting down her hairbrush, Jenna rushed to answer
her bedroom phone before it shattered Aunt Molly's
sleep. She checked the caller ID window and answered
hopefully. "Beau?"

"Hi," he said. "I'm just checking in to make sure all's
well. My errands are taking longer than expected."

Jenna's spirits took another nose dive. He sounded
tense—or distant. "We're fine."

"Good. I picked up the solvent, and I'm heading for
home now. I might be longer than a half hour."

"No problem. Take your time."

"Okay. See you soon."

Swallowing the knot in her throat, Jenna replaced the
handset, then returned to the bathroom to finish brushing her hair. She'd changed from her jeans and sweatshirt into black socks, flats and leggings, and topped
them with a long white cable-knit sweater with a deep
cowl neckline. She pulled a few bangs onto her forehead. Small gold hoops shone from her earlobes, and a
matching gold-filigreed, rose-quartz-and-onyx pendant
hung from a gold chain around her neck.

But all of her efforts were for nothing, she thought
as she left her room and moved into the hall. No matter
what Aunt Molly said *haute couture* wouldn't change
the way Beau felt about her now. The only way she'd
be able to regain the trust they'd once had was to—

Glass shattered, and nerves rioting, Jenna ran for the

foyer as the piercing security alarm erupted in a pulsing cacophony that nearly split her eardrums. She got to the wide archway just as a short thin man wearing a stocking mask clambered through the smashed side light on the front door and dropped to the floor. Everything happened in split seconds.

Jenna ran for the staircase. She had to protect Aunt Molly! But the small man had already unlocked the door, and a taller intruder in a stocking mask burst inside while the short one took a baseball bat to the security keypad, silencing the alarm.

Jenna scrambled up the stairs. Halfway up, the tall man grabbed her ankles and suddenly she was airborne—crashing down on the steps. He dragged her to him. Fighting the pain, she twisted, turned! Got one foot free and kicked his kneecap. With a guttural cry, he fell on top of her. Jenna clawed at the face behind the nylon mask—went for his eyes, tried to bring her knee to his groin. Now the other man was on her, too, forcing a foul-smelling rag over her nose and mouth.

Chloroform! *Help me Father!*

The last few words she heard before she lost consciousness was Aunt Molly yelling, "You let her be!" and the tall man shouting that Jenna was supposed to be alone. Then he said something that made her fight harder, though her head was spinning and she was drowning in the blackness. *"Take care of the old lady. I'll get this one in the van."*

Beau's cell phone chimed as he took a set of kneepads from a hook in his shop, and he set them down on his workbench. He was instantly afraid when he heard Fish Troutman's grave voice.

"Beau, it's Fish. I don't have much time to talk, but

Mrs. Jennings gave me your cell phone number and in-sisted that I call."

If there was a problem, why wasn't Aunt Molly call-ing? Why wasn't Jenna? "Fish?"

"Jenna was taken. Fifteen or twenty minutes ago."

How could that be? He'd just spoken to her! "What do you mean, she was taken? Taken from the inn?"

"Yes. Now before you get too—"

"Who took her?"

"Two men in stocking masks. The state police are setting up check points on all the roads leading out of town."

The bottom fell out of Beau's stomach. In twenty minutes she could be in the next county. In forty-five minutes, she could be on the interstate traveling at sixty-five miles an hour toward God knew where! He kept his phone to his ear as he ran to his truck. "Okay, you've said what the PSP are doing. What are *you* doing to find her?"

"What we need to do—looking for evidence that'll help us locate her."

Of course they were, and he shouldn't be taking out his frustration on Fish. He started the engine, dropped the truck in gear and roared out of his driveway. He should've been with her. He'd made a promise! Sud-denly, he realized he hadn't asked about Aunt Molly, then did.

"She's on her way to the hospital. One of the perps banged her up a little."

"What?"

"Not intentionally. He shoved her in a closet and wedged a chair under the knob. She says she's okay, though."

Thank God for that. "What else do you know?"

"Beau, I need to go."

"Just the basics."

"Okay. Elmer Fox came by about ten minutes after the abduction to drop off some photographs and saw that four-foot side light smashed out of the front door. When he yelled through the opening, Mrs. Jennings yelled back. He went inside, got her out, then tried to call the station. But the perps had cut the phone line before they broke in, obviously so the security company wasn't alerted. If Jenna'd had a wireless system that wouldn't have worked. Anyway, Mrs. Jennings called us from her cell phone."

Beau flicked on his wipers. The snow was thin and grainy, coating the roads and adding to the accumulation on the berms. He was approaching the strip mall now, and scanning every passing car and truck. "What kind of vehicle are you looking for?"

"We don't know yet. I'm on my way out the door now to help Drago. We're canvassing the neighborhood while Perris handles things here."

"Fish, I need to help."

"You can't. Just pray and stay available, and I'll let you know when we hear something. Bye."

Sick to his soul, Beau tucked his phone away and kept driving toward town because there was nothing else he could do.

He'd never felt so helpless and afraid in his life.

FOURTEEN

Jenna fought the dream, fought the numbing cold. Beau was swinging that axe again, hacking at logs for a fire. Everything would be okay, he insisted. She'd be warm soon. But it wasn't okay. She could barely feel her hands and feet, and the nausea and dizziness were getting worse.

Her eyes flew open in a rush of horror. This was real! The cold, the men in stocking masks, the drug-induced nausea! Dear God, she'd been brought here and left to die!

But where was *here,* and how could she get away with her hands tied behind her back and her ankles bound?

She rolled to her knees—tried to stand. The effort brought her slamming to the ground and crying out in pain. She got to her knees again and through a wave of nausea, took stock of her situation. She was in a wooded valley, in the middle of a roofless, three-walled, crumbling stone structure. All around her tall pines and bare tree limbs caught the snow that continued to fall. She swallowed the bile rising in her throat. Hypothermia was a certainty—her sweater, leggings and suede flats wouldn't stop it. Death was a terrifying possibility.

Frantic, shaking uncontrollably, she glanced around, then moved toward the only shelter available.

Two of the long gray stone walls created a corner, approximately ten feet at its highest, then gradually decreased to four feet. There was a hole in the third wall where a door had once been. She moved toward the corner, praying for help, snow-covered rocks and clumps threatening her balance and cutting into her knees.

Her labored gasps fogged the air. She knew where she was now. This was The Hideaway, the old turn-of-the-century railroad depot near Payton's Rocks that Beau had told her about.

Beau!

Feelings of betrayal crushed her heart for a second, but in the next, she knew he'd never hurt her. He was everything good in this world. The men who'd broken in had to have learned about The Hideaway from the bugs at the Blackberry.

"Please, help me," she prayed, trying not to cry and continuing to make her way over the uneven ground. People had to be looking for her—the police, friends, Beau. Aunt Molly had seen the men. She'd tell the authorities who to—

Jenna stopped abruptly. Now her tears did come. How could she have forgotten that Aunt Molly had been in danger, too? "Oh, dear Jesus, please let her be okay. Don't let them have hurt her."

The sound of a vehicle—distant, but coming closer—reached Jenna's ears, and suddenly hope rose her chest. "Help!" she cried. "I'm down here!" Her thoughts sped along. Maybe someone had heard the alarm—given the police a description of the van they'd used. Maybe her abductors had been caught and told Perris where to find her!

The engine sounds ceased and in desperation she cried out again. But when no reply came after minutes of constant shouting, Jenna had to accept that help wasn't coming.

She'd begun to move toward that stone corner again when she heard the unmistakable roar of a snowmobile or all-terrain vehicle. Someone *was* coming for her! "Thank you, God," she whispered. "Thank you."

One bright headlight pierced the grainy veil of falling snow. "Here!" she called jubilantly. "I'm here!"

The light came closer, the engine louder. She could make out the shape of the snowmobile and the rider now. Beau!

He stopped twenty yards away on the rise above her, then slowly got off the sled and descended the brush and sapling-covered ground toward her. And a new chill took away her last bit of warmth. The tall man in the dark topcoat and gray plaid muffler picking his way through the fine snow and brush wasn't here to save her. He was here to kill her.

Beau parked his truck in the Charity PD's lot and strode into the station. He'd spoken to a nurse in the ER and learned that Aunt Molly would be fine. Now all he could do was pray that Jenna would be okay, too. He loved her. There was no denying it anymore. No more flip-flopping about what was best for either of them. He loved her with every breath in his body, and he didn't know how he could live through this nightmare if she didn't.

Flame-haired, middle-aged dispatcher Sarah French

bustled around her desk to hug him. They weren't usually hugging friends, but he sensed that she needed to "comfort," and he accepted her affectionate squeeze gratefully. Despite her flamboyant style—the royal blue pantsuit, half-dozen carnival glass necklaces and dangling gold fish earrings—she was dependable, smart and savvy.

"Fish thought you'd be coming by," she said. "Charlie's on his way in to mind the store, but he won't care if you hang out here for a while." Eagerness to help shone in the blue eyes behind her red-framed glasses. "Sit. I'll get you a cup of coffee. Or would you rather have cocoa? We have some of those packets that you mix with hot water."

"Thanks, Sarah, but I'm okay." His stomach was burning, and caffeine would only increase the acid sloshing around in there. "I'll take that seat, though." Beau sank to a folding chair along the wall. Then he closed his eyes and prayed.

Jenna didn't know how she found the courage to defy him, but as he stepped across the jagged rocks to tower over her, she refused to show fear.

"Well, well," he said easily, "what have we here?"

She looked up into Courtland Dane's smug, ice-blue eyes. They were the same, no longer hidden behind tinted glasses. The flawlessly trimmed mustache and close-to-the-jaw beard were the same, too. But his nose was broader and his cheekbones were more prominent. He'd had cosmetic surgery while he'd been underground. His hair was pulled back from his forehead in a short ponytail, and a diamond stud shone from his right earlobe. The limping man from the diner was unmasked.

"You ruined my life," he said cordially.

"You ruined your own life."

He ignored her reply. "I have to say it, Jenna. You looked much better the last time I saw you. Radiant. Beautiful. And now..." He shrugged. "But, no matter. I only want to talk to you—nothing else, since I'm not interested in the carpenter's leftovers."

He seemed to expect a denial from her, but she remained silent.

He gestured smoothly with black-gloved hands. "Nothing to say? Not even a plea for mercy? Or a blanket? Well, then, do let me get the conversation going— catch you up with what's been going on in my life. Isn't that what friends do when they haven't seen each other for a time?"

He smiled. "Where have I been?" he asked, then said, "Thank you for asking, I've been living in Barbados, though I can't say I enjoyed it." He touched his nose, his cheek. "I wasn't particularly fond of the surgery, either, but it was a necessary evil that—along with some nicely made credentials—allowed me to return to the States last month." He walked around as though he were taking a summer stroll while grainy snow continued to fall. "Of course, as Thomas Wolfe said, you can't really go home again.

"Are you cold, Jenna? Can you still feel your feet? Your hands? I've done some reading on hypothermia that you might find interesting. Taking into account the amount of time you've been here, you'll soon begin to lose focus and hallucinate. Then your movements will become clumsy and uncoordinated. Although," he chuckled softly, "you seem to have reached that point out of sequence." He continued to slowly circle her.

"Eventually you'll wish you'd died the night you made me cut you."

She couldn't remain silent any longer. "I didn't *make* you cut me! You did that on your own."

Dane flew into a rage—knocked her to the ground. "I was entitled to compensation! You were mine, and you let that young miscreant touch you!"

Jenna fired back though her pain, refused to right herself because that meant kneeling in front of him. "I was never yours! And he did nothing but help me—"

"Oh, I know how he helped you," Dane returned viciously. "I saw it on his face when he left."

He took a moment to calm himself, then brushed snow from the lapels of his topcoat and raised his chin, once more the polished power broker. "You took away what I valued most in this world. While I still have wealth, I'll never be able to return to my station in the financial community. Now it will give me great pleasure to know you'll end your days in misery as well.

"Of course, my unhappiness will be tempered by the fact that I'll still be breathing." Smiling, he withdrew a small GPS from his pocket, flashed it, then returned it to his coat. "How fitting that your lover supplied the perfect place for your death." He paused to adjust his scarf, then smiled again. "Goodbye, Jenna. Don't get up. I'll show myself out."

Raw fear splintered through her, accompanied by a staggering sense of desperation. But she wouldn't call him back, wouldn't beg for her life because she knew it was what he wanted.

She waited until she heard the snowmobile's engine roar to life. Then she got to her knees again and made her way through the snow to the corner of the ruins. Wedging herself into the crook, then moving up and down against the rocks, she managed to manipulate her sweater's deep cowl neckline up to partially cover her head. It wouldn't preserve much of her remaining body heat, but it would help. And she would keep moving her fingers and toes—keep living. Beau would come for her. He would remember what they'd talked about while they were being recorded, and with God's help he would find her.

She looked into the falling snow where a small portion of milky sky showed between the tall pines and hemlocks, and she whispered the Lord's Prayer.

It was so hard to say, "Thy will be done."

For the fourth time, the phone rang at the station and for the fourth time Beau leapt to his feet. This time, when Charlie Banks answered the phone, he didn't send Beau a bleak look and shake his head.

Beau heard him speak over the news on CNN and the hum of the copy machine where Sarah was working. Banks was a heavyset, grandfatherly man with rimless bifocals, and gray walrus mustache, but the gruffness in his voice always made him sound like he was half ticked off.

"Good," he said. "Is Perris handling it? Do you need anything from me? Traffic control? Okay, then I'll stay here." He looked at Beau. "Yeah, I'll tell him."

Beau was through the low gate dividing the office from the reception area by the time Charlie hung up. "Did they find her?"

"No, but Fish thinks he's got the fella who took her. His rental car slid off the road out by the strip mall and smacked into a stone abutment."

"He's alive and talking?"

"Yeah, but he's not bein' cooperative. They're waitin' for the ambulance."

Beau headed for the door. This wasn't the news he'd prayed for, but it was *something*.

Charlie called out to him. "You won't be welcome out there, but I expect you need to go. Careful on those roads."

The snow kept falling as Beau passed the burning flares on the highway and pulled onto the side of the road behind a police cruiser. Fish and Drago were just handing over traffic control to a couple of firemen. Above the road, in the mall's parking lot, a few curiosity seekers looked down on the accident. Leaving his truck, Beau sprinted across the road to where Chief Perris stood beside a late-model black sedan. The driver's door was open, and a man in a black topcoat was leaning back against the headrest holding a cloth to his forehead. His right wrist was handcuffed to the steering wheel.

Perris took two long strides to halt Beau's progress. "Go back to the station and wait. I'll let you know—"

He was sick of hearing that people would "let him know." Beau shouldered past Perris—heard the chief bark, "Troutman, get a leash on your friend!" But nothing could keep him from the face he'd seen on his computer screen. The slightly modified face stared back. Despite his injuries, the powerbroker with the ice-blue eyes managed a slow, smug smile that amplified Beau's anger and made him consider things he'd never done before.

Dane spoke smoothly over the ambulance's screaming arrival, ridicule in his voice. "Hello, Carpenter."

"Where is she?" Beau demanded.

Lowering the bloody cloth, he said cordially, "I don't know what you're talking about."

Fish took his arm. "Come on, Beau. You need to step back."

"And you need to make this idiot talk!"

"Troutman, get him out of there!" Perris yelled as he went to meet the paramedics.

"Come on, Beau!"

Dane repeated Beau's question. "Where is she? *If* I had anything to do with her disappearance, which I did not, I'd guess that she's—" he smiled "—*hidden away* somewhere. Though I doubt you'll find her in time." His tone cooled. "Just know that your little harlot got what she deserved."

Beau lunged for him, caught the lapels of Dane's top-coat before he dragged him back. But in those few seconds before he wrestled him away, Beau saw something that gave him hope. There was a handheld GPS on the Chrysler's console—and the car was already equipped with one!

Thoughts racing, he stared from several yards away at Dane's light gray dress pants. They were wet up to his calves, which implied that he'd either been walking where the snow was deeper—or where snow-covered brush could leave it's mark.

Fish was still beside him, repeatedly assuring him that they'd find Jenna. But Beau was only half listening. He had to think.

It was agony to wait until the paramedics fitted Dane with a collar and transferred him to a gurney, but the instant he was in the ambulance, Beau turned to Fish. "I need a favor."

Fish glanced back at Perris who was talking to Drago now. "No."

"Listen," he said earnestly. "There's a GPS lying on the Chrysler's console. I need to see it."

Fish shook his head. "Perris'll skin me."

The reprisal would probably be a lot worse than that, but— "Please. Just get it and check the coordinates listed. The car has a factory-installed navigation system. There's no need for Dane to have a spare GPS unless he planned to head for another destination on foot." He lowered his voice when Perris sent them a suspicious glance. "Please. It'll be dark soon, and the temperature's dropping. Jenna could be at one of those coordinates."

The air in front of Fish steamed when he sighed. "Okay. This is Perris's collar, so he'll be following the ambulance to the ER, and leaving Drago and me to clean up here and wait for the wrecker. But you're gonna owe me big-time."

"Whatever you want is yours."

"Yeah, right. Just put on your gloves, and don't screw up our perp's fingerprints."

Two minutes later Beau was staring at the GPS's lighted display, his nerve endings on fire. There was only one latitude and longitude listed—only one waypoint. He headed for his truck. "Fish, I need to borrow this for a while."

Fish rushed after him. "No! You can't have that!"

Knowing Fish couldn't stop him without getting himself in hot water, Beau climbed inside, slammed the door and started the engine. It was unfair, but it wasn't life-or-death. Jenna's circumstances were. "I'll bring it back!" he shouted through his closed side window.

"Beau!"

Hitting the gas, he fishtailed around the police cruiser in front of him, then headed south toward Payton's Rocks, the direction from which Dane had come. Beau kept one eye on the road and the other on the GPS's lighted display. The arrow directed him to take a left turn onto an old state route. And suddenly, Beau knew—*hoped and prayed that he knew*—where Dane had left her. He'd said Jenna was probably "hidden away" somewhere. Was that a sly little clue from a not-so-clever egomaniac? Dane had had the Blackberry bugged. He had to have heard Beau telling Jenna about The Hideaway.

It was misery driving only fast enough for conditions. But the salt trucks had been out, and here and there the salt was doing its job. Signs of residential life disappeared as he climbed higher into the Alleghenies, passing hunting camps, his heart beating faster with every mile.

He glanced at the GPS to be sure, but he already knew his destination was just over the next rise. "Thank you, God," he whispered. "Please, don't let me be too late."

He spotted a snowmobile in the twilight, sitting at the head end of the old railroad grade. Beau yanked his cell phone from his belt.

Sarah French answered his 911 call. "Sarah, it's Beau. I need an ambulance. I'm six miles from town on State Route 549, about a mile past the road leading to Payton's Rocks. My truck will be there."

"Did you find her?"

If he was wrong, he'd worry about it later. "Yes. Hurry!"

Grabbing the old blanket and flashlight he kept for emergencies from his backseat, he ran for the snowmobile, half skidding, half falling in the snow. "Please, please," he whispered. He hopped on the sled—thanked

God that the key was still in the ignition. Seconds later, he was roaring through the blowing snow toward the old depot. Two jarring, interminably long minutes later, the ruins were below him. Beau parked the sled, grabbed the flashlight and blanket, and crashed down through the uneven terrain and brush toward those decaying walls.

"Jenna!"

No answer. He called her name again. Still nothing.

Fear of what he'd find took his breath as those stone walls came closer. He was only twenty yards away now…ten yards…five. He rushed inside. Blood thudded in his temples as he glanced around. Then with a muffled cry, he spotted her, nearly snow-covered in the high corner. He was beside her in a moment, brushing snow from her cold face and hair and releasing her bonds. He wrapped her in the blanket from her head to her feet—pulled her onto his lap and slid his warm gloves over her frozen hands. "Jenna! Jenna, wake up!"

Unzipping his jacket, he pulled her against his warm chest, rubbed her blanket-covered back and limbs. Tears stung his eyes. "Jenna, please wake up. Stay with me. Because I don't know what I'll do if you leave." He kissed her cheeks, brushed wet hair from her face, kissed her lips.

Then a sigh broke between them, and every terrified muscle Beau owned sagged in relief.

A hint of a smile touched her lips as her eyes finally opened. "Relax," she whispered. "I'm not going anywhere without you."

That wasn't entirely true.

After he'd carried her to the snowmobile, then to his heated truck, Fish, Perris and the ambulance arrived, and the paramedics took her away. Beau had followed in his truck, praying constantly that Dane and the elements hadn't done irreversible damage. He knew about hypothermia. It could cost limbs, heart problems, even death.

He was pacing outside the emergency room when he heard Jenna raise her voice and refuse to give Perris a statement until Beau was in the room. Red-faced again, the chief opened the door and beckoned him inside.

She was fully alert when he eased inside the privacy curtain. It killed him to see her scrapes and bruises and the IV line in her left hand. But she was alive. Jenna slid her right hand out from her warming blankets to take his.

"You look better," he said, smiling.

"Warmer and drier, anyway. Thanks to you."

He shook his head and pointed skyward.

"I know," she said quietly. "Him, too." Then Beau listened while she gave Perris the statement he wanted.

When Perris and Fish were gone, Beau took a seat at the side of her narrow bed. They'd started something wonderful in the ruins. Now he wanted to make that permanent. Nearly losing her had hammered home the point that life was short, and only a fool wasted a moment of it.

He stroked her hand and spoke softly. "I want to say a lot of things right now, but first I need to know if you remember what you said at the ruins."

Jenna sent him a hesitant smile. "I said I wasn't going anywhere without you. Did you mean what you said?"

"Oh, yeah." He considered what he was about to say for a moment—tried to find the right words and failed so he did the best he could. "I know you'll probably want to take this slow. I mean, this is all pretty new. But when the time's right I have a question to ask you."

Against his protests, she sat up on the bed and inched a little closer. "Maybe you should ask me now, while I still have the courage to say a few things to you."

"What things?"

"I have scars from the attack. They're not terrible... but they're there."

How could she think that mattered to him? "So what?"

"I might not be able to give you a baby."

Careful of her IV, he gathered her close. "I don't know how important that is to you, but it isn't to me. A baby of our own would be great. But I didn't fall in love with the idea of having a child. I fell in love with you. After growing up the way I did, I'd almost prefer to adopt a kid who needs a couple of good parents and a loving home."

Tears welled in her eyes. "Maybe we'll be able to do both."

"Maybe we will," he repeated. Then smiling again, he tipped her face up to his. "Now will you please say yes so we can get on with the kissing part of this proposal?"

Jenna laughed softly. "Yes," she whispered as he bent to cover her lips. "Yes, yes, yes."

EPILOGUE

Jenna looked out the window at the gently falling snow beyond St. John's filled-to-capacity parking lot. Today the late-March snow didn't frighten her. It was no longer a terrifying instrument of death. It was a lovely white backdrop to the happiest day of her life.

Margo and Rachel came to the window to fuss with the train of her simple white satin gown and the crown of pink rosettes and ivy circling her head.

"Remind you of anything?" Margo asked, grinning.

Jenna grinned back. A little over a year ago, the three of them had gathered in this same room to fuss over Margo before her wedding to Cole. Now, dressed in strapless, spring-green satin gowns and carrying nosegays of pink roses, baby's breath and ivy, Rachel and Margo were doing the same for her.

"This is so incredible," Jenna said, her gaze moving between her two best friends. "Two years ago, the three of us were all single and wondering if we'd ever find someone to build a life with." She hugged Margo. "Now you and Cole are together—" she hugged Rachel "—you and Jake are expecting a baby, and in a few minutes, Beau and I will be saying our vows."

Rachel smiled. "We're all so blessed."

Jenna nodded. The dangers in their lives were in the past now. Thanks to Courtland's testimony, he and the men who'd abducted her were in prison. As for "Mrs. Bolton"… She was still out there, but Jenna didn't fear her return.

Gayle Harper stepped inside, a smile on her young-looking features. She wore a lacy beige mother-of-the-bride dress, and her ash-blond hair was arranged in the same softly upswept style as Jenna's—wispy bangs, loose, face-framing tendrils and all. She walked to Jenna and kissed her, happy tears shining in her eyes. Then she took in the three of them. "Ready?" she asked. "There are three good-looking young men out there waiting for you to join them."

"And one of them," Aunt Molly added peeking inside, "is getting very impatient to see his bride."

Rachel placed a bouquet of trailing white lilies, pink roses and ivy in Jenna's hands, then kissed her cheek. "Well then, let's not keep him waiting a minute longer."

Margo kissed Jenna's other cheek, a tradition that had begun at her wedding. "You *are* ready, right?"

Filled with indescribable joy, Jenna nodded. "I've been ready forever."

With his nerve endings vibrating with every soft note filling the church, Beau watched Margo, then Rachel glide down the church's white runner, smiling at friends, then joining their husbands to stand to the left of Reverend Landers. If Jenna didn't show up soon, he'd come completely apart. He didn't know how much more tension he could take.

His heart shot into his throat when the organ music stopped.

Then Emma Lucille hit a few high notes, started the

wedding march and the congregation stood to face the back of the church.

All of Beau's jitters fell away as Jenna appeared and walked slowly forward with her mom on her right and Aunt Molly on her left.

How could he have ever considered backing away from her? How could he have even tried? She was perfection from the roses in her hair to the cross at her throat and the snow-white gown that left her shoulders bare.

He stepped out to meet her, and everything around him faded to a blur except for her beautiful face.

"Last chance to back out," Jenna whispered, and there was so much love in her blue eyes Beau was afraid his voice would break when he answered.

"Not a chance," he whispered back. Smiling, he brought her fingertips to his lips and kissed them. "Not a chance in Heaven."

* * * * *

Dear Reader,

We live in amazing times.

Wireless cell phones connect us with distant friends and family; the internet feeds us information in seconds; and robots sometimes do the work of people on assembly lines. God has blessed us with an incredible amount of intelligence.

But there was a time when the world didn't spin quite as fast. Understand, I'd miss my computer and cell phone if I didn't have them. But back in the 1950s and 1960s, penny candy, soda fountains and kick-the-can on warm summer nights were the highlights of our young lives.

Mike and I talked about that as we sipped slushies, munched popcorn and watched an international bunch of kids play baseball at the 2011 Little League World Series in Williamsport, Pennsylvania. Being there was a gentle reminder to enjoy the simpler things in life. That afternoon, no one in the stands "texted" or "tweeted" their smiles and applause. They cheered, they clapped and they chanted. It was personal. And it was great. God willing, we'll be there again in August!

Blessings,
Lauren

Questions for Discussion

1. In the recent past, Jenna was a jury foreperson. If you've ever served on a jury, how did it feel, having someone's life in your hands? Did you ask God for guidance? Did you consider excusing yourself because the responsibility was too great?

2. During a Sunday church service, Jenna's pastor tells his congregation that when we've done as much as we can to solve a problem, we have to give it to God and move on. Sometimes that's easier said than done. How do you deal with situations over which you have no control?

3. As a teenager, Beau had a scrape with the law, and Aunt Molly paid his fines under two conditions: He was to work off his debt, and start attending church. Eventually Beau wanted to attend—but is there a better way to introduce non-believers to Jesus? Have you ever tried to do that, and what was the outcome?

4. Who is your favorite secondary character in this book, and why?

5. One of the characters in *At Any Cost* is octogenarian Elmer Fox who has definite opinions about today's fads. What are your views on current fashions, tattoos and piercings? Do you agree with Elmer? Or do you accept that we're all different and have a right to live our lives as we see fit?

6. There are dream sequences in this book. Some people believe that dreams have a purpose beyond entertaining us while we sleep. What do you think?

7. Jenna reads from her Bible most nights before retiring, particularly from the Book of Psalms. Do you have a favorite book or a scripture passage that speaks to you?

8. Jealousy and revenge motivate the villain in this book. Several references in the Bible advise us to take "an eye for an eye." Yet in the Lord's prayer, we're urged to forgive those who hurt us. As Christians, can we live our lives both ways?

9. Regardless of Jenna and Aunt Molly's trust in him, Beau—in the role of protector—refuses to stay in the bed-and-breakfast with Jenna while Aunt Molly's away for a few days. He's been the brunt of gossip and doesn't want Jenna touched by it. Considering that Beau and Jenna would've been sleeping on different floors, was he being too chivalrous? Or must we always avoid the appearance of wrongdoing?

10. Aunt Molly tells Beau and Jenna that her late husband's philosophy regarding gossips was simple. If they were talking about him, they were leaving someone else alone. Is that realistic?

11. At the end of the book when Jenna prays that God will spare her life, she says the Lord's Prayer and finds it difficult to say four words. What are they? Has it ever been hard for you to say those words?

INSPIRATIONAL

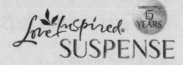

Love Inspired® SUSPENSE

celebrating 15 YEARS

COMING NEXT MONTH
AVAILABLE MAY 8, 2012

LOST LEGACY
Treasure Seekers
Dana Mentink

THE BLACK SHEEP'S REDEMPTION
Fitzgerald Bay
Lynette Eason

IDENTITY CRISIS
Laura Scott

FATAL DISCLOSURE
Sandra Robbins

LISCNM0412

REQUEST YOUR FREE BOOKS!

2 FREE RIVETING INSPIRATIONAL NOVELS
PLUS 2 FREE MYSTERY GIFTS

Love Inspired®
SUSPENSE

When Brooke McKaslin returns to Montana on family business, she has no intention of forming any new relationships, especially with a man like Liam Knightly. But things don't always go according to plan....

Here's a sneak peek at MONTANA HOMECOMING by Jillian Hart.

"What's your story?" Brooke asked.

"Which story do you want to know?"

"Why adding a dog to your life has been your biggest commitment to date."

"How many relationships do you know that have stood the test of time?" Oscar rushed up to him, panting hard, his prize clamped between his teeth. Liam scrubbed the dog's head.

"Ooh, tough question." She wrestled with that one herself. "My parents are divorced. My father has divorced twice. The twins' mother has been in and out of marriages."

"My parents are divorced, too. Although they both live in Washington, D.C."

"The lawyers?"

"Both workaholics. Both are Type A."

"Things you inherited?"

"Mostly." He tugged his keys from his pocket, the parking lot nearer now. "Maybe I inherited the bad marriage gene."

"I know the feeling."

"That's why you're still single?"

"One reason." The truth sat on the tip of her tongue, ready to be told. What was she doing? She swallowed hard, holding back the words. What was it about Liam that made her guards weaken? She'd nearly opened up to him. She shook her head. No way did she know him enough to trust him. "It's my opinion men cause destruction and ruin wherever they go."

"Funny, that's my opinion about women." His slow grin made her heart skip a beat.

Good thing her heart wasn't in charge. She was. And she wasn't going to let his stunning smile weaken her defenses any further. Time to shore them up. She hiked her chin and steeled her spine.

"I know that's not fair." Liam winked. "But that's how it feels."

So hard to ignore that wink. She let it bounce off her, unaffected. She'd gotten as close to him as she was going to. Best to remember she worked for him, she was leaving as soon as the trial was over and the last thing she wanted was a man to complicate things. She had a life again. No way was she going to mess that up.

You'll love the rest of MONTANA HOMECOMING,
from one of your favorite authors, Jillian Hart,
available May 2012 from Love Inspired®.

SHLIEXP0512